Limited Run

Three Women in a Play

Mia Nadasi

Published in the United Kingdom by Thalia44
Cover design by J Ferd

ISBN 9781471633447

Also by Mia Nadasi

Pirouettes and Passions
Growing up Behind the Curtain

"This is a fabulous autobiographical account ... a really worthwhile read." *(Dance Europe)*

"It is the vivid confessional tone of the memoir that grips." *(Plays International)*

"Movies will make you famous. Television will make you rich. But the theatre will make you good."

(Terrence Mann actor/director)

PART ONE

Prologue

"Ladies and gentlemen, tonight's performance of *Uncle Vanya* will commence at 7.30. This is your half hour call." The stage manager's voice comes over the tannoy.

Even though this is not a surprise, it makes Bella's stomach contract.

Tonight's performance would be the first in front of an audience. In the old regional theatres, this would have been the First Night, the Première, but nowadays they don't allow the critics into the theatre at the beginning of the run, so tonight's performance is the first preview. Not that that makes Bella breathe any easier. She hasn't been on stage for twelve years. She doesn't want to think of this. There is no point in thinking of this. Concentrate on the hair.

She looks into the dressing table mirror, but the sight doesn't bring her solace. The hair is up in a loose chignon, but Bella thinks it makes her look older. Normally she has a sharp, short haircut, but since they are doing the play in the period it was written, thank God, it means she has to have a hairpiece attached. Everyone said at the first dress rehearsal that she looked lovely but at this moment she is not convinced. The face looking back at her is a stranger's.

There is a knock on the door and the stage door keeper arrives with another bouquet of flowers. Bella already has two large vases full, but her heart leaps. Maybe this will be the one. She thanks the young lady, takes the flowers, and opens the little envelope attached; it is from her agent. Her heart sinks — this wasn't the one she had been hoping for.

Maybe he had sent her a card. She looks through the numerous good luck cards she'd opened earlier. A funny one from Storm, who plays Sonia — a bit vulgar, probably not suitable for an older colleague but she is young; a formal picture of flowers from Evelyn, who plays Vanya's mother. Women are always better at organising themselves in these sorts of things, Bella thinks. On the other hand, Uncle Vanya, the star actor of the production, sent her a bouquet of yellow roses. He even put: *to match the beautiful dress in Act II you look so stunning in.*

But nothing from **him.**

Her thought is interrupted, as there is a knock on the door and at the same time Storm flies in. "Sorry, sorry," she shouts, "I know I shouldn't disturb you when you are getting into character, but do you have any hairspray? I forgot to bring mine."

Bella hands her the hairspray; she squirts it liberally on her ponytail, which hangs down on her back, and all over her escaping tendrils of hair. "Bless you, thank you, good luck," she says with a beaming smile, and takes off again.

Unbelievable, thinks Bella; maybe her parents knew something when she was born. How else would you call a baby Storm? She picks up the hairspray and gives an extra puff to her hairpiece.

The stage manager calls the quarter; that means the play will begin in twenty minutes. Her character, Yelena, is on in the first ten minutes. These are the worst moments. Why am I doing this to myself? After all these years, why did I want to get back on stage? She hopes the attack of nerves will pass once the play starts.

She rises from her mirror with a deep sigh, and at the same moment the door bursts open and Gabriel, who plays Astrov, stands there with a slightly battered bunch of flowers, the kind you often see at garages in a bucket. Gabriel grins, "You thought I'd forgotten, didn't you?" "Well," she says "we are on in a moment. You, even before me. "

But Gabriel gives her a big bear hug, slams the flowers down, "Good luck, my angel," he says with that slight Irish lilt she finds so irresistible, turns back from the door, shouts: "Sock it to them," and is out of the dressing room.

Bella can't breathe for a moment; maybe the corset is too tight. She peels the cellophane off and puts the flowers in the vase. She feels her confidence seeping back—she got the flowers she was waiting for. No card, though, which she could have saved. That would have been nice, but this is better than nothing.

She turns back to the mirror and powders her lips, an action she never forgets ever since, as a young actress, she was told off because she'd smeared her leading man with bright red lipstick during a kissing scene. So unprofessional, she was told. Sadly, there is only the one kiss between Yelena and Astrov. The lips are less shiny now. The show can begin.

Bella

Six months earlier

Unfortunately, the old image of the actor waiting for the phone to ring had become all too real for Bella lately. She was well known for her television work; in fact, the whole country knew her from her long-running series, which ended only a couple of years ago. Now, nobody would offer her a lesser role on television than that of a 'leading lady'. But customarily, in each TV production, there is only one leading lady, and Bella was just a year short of her fiftieth birthday — not the traditional leading lady age.

Not that she'd been desperate. She'd always had plenty of personal appearances, interviews, fashion shoots; and generally, she was kept busy. In addition, she never missed her exercise classes twice a week and quite enjoyed pottering around her comfortable bourgeois home.

Her husband, twelve years her senior, was an academic. He was quietly supportive of Bella's career but didn't like the limelight. The new celebrity culture was alien to him; he preferred to stay in the background.

The marriage functioned well: they respected each other's space and often their work took them to different surroundings.

Long gone were the days when the young, impressionable actress had met the thirty something university lecturer, man of the world with a shining intellect, who swept her off her feet. Though the rest of the world called him Theo, Bella addressed him as Theodor, his full name seeming to fit him better in Bella's eyes. Their romance had been short, and they had married within a year of meeting, despite the advice of some agents and casting directors who believed that marriage would hinder Bella's career. In those days, there were some producers who liked to employ pretty, young actresses who were unattached.

The advice proved wrong because Bella became a success on television early in her career. She had a face the camera loved. Large saucer eyes, sweeping eyelashes, full lips — before the fashion of Botox made gaping fish faces of the influencers of social media. Bella worked continuously — one series followed another — and soon her face was recognised countrywide. Occasionally, she took stage roles as well, just to stay grounded, as she liked to say, but those paled in significance compared to her high-visibility television parts.

The last ten years, though, had been quieter and the gaps between the jobs had grown each time a bit longer. Yes, she had to admit that the telephone did not ring so often.

Then this. Out of the blue, her agent called and asked her if she fancied some theatre work in the provinces. The play was Chekhov's *Uncle Vanya* and the role—the young wife of a professor, the object of desire of every man in the play.

Her instinct was to say yes, immediately, but her agent, who knew her better than she knew herself, said she ought to think about it. Would she want to spend at least two months in a small place called Maidenford? Does she want to return to the stage after a twelve-year break and does she think that the part of Yelena is right for her? What the agent did not say was that Yelena is in her twenties in the play, an age Bella passed a long time ago. But he had more tact than to mention it. He suggested they wait a few days before giving an answer, there being no urgency, since the dates were six months ahead.

Bella's world turned upside down: she couldn't sleep and she lost her appetite. One moment, she was excited at the prospect of taking up the challenge, the next she thought herself too old for the part and was afraid she would fail dismally. She had a reputation to protect. On the other hand, to go back to the theatre, most actors' first love and priority, and appear in a masterpiece, was too tempting.

In the second phone call to her agent, she enquired about the director and the cast. The answers were satisfying, especially as the renowned actor, Auberon Hayman, was to play Vanya. That would secure national press, said her agent. More at stake, so, possibly, there was more to gain.

Responding to her fear about the age of the character, her agent said that the director's approach was to cast the ever-desirable woman. In his opinion, that was someone with the charisma of Bella. Bella was flattered and did not hesitate longer. "I'll do it," she said, and she felt ecstatic.

But as the date approached, her anxiety grew. What have I done? How could I have thought I would be able to do that? I will make myself ridiculous. The critics will tear me apart.

Theodor, who rarely interfered with her choices, seeing her indecision, sat her down and counselled her. "If you don't take the challenge, you will regret it forever. If it's not a success, then nothing has changed. but if it reveals another side of you, it could open new doors. Say the National Theatre?"

He knew that Bella thought of the National as a company that could put a stamp of greatness on an actor. Bella saw reason in the argument. She would take the challenge, she would. She would be the best Yelena in living memory!

Storm

Four months before opening night

Storm looked around her untidy room. The last few weeks had been wildly uplifting, scary, joyful, desperate in equal measure. She'd finished her drama school training, and the last performances had taken place. She'd said goodbye to her closest friends, the ones she had lived and breathed with for three years, and now...Who knew if they would ever see each other again?

She had to do something about her room. There were dirty cups and food remnants all over, even on the shelves among the books, which were mostly plays she was studying. A gentle, thin layer of dust covered everything. The window hadn't been cleaned for three years, she was thinking to herself. She weighed up the risk of falling two floors if she attempted to clean the outside.

Storm was the first member of her family to have any artistic leanings. She came from a working-class family in the provinces, and though her mother took her to ballet classes in the local church hall, she was most surprised that the little girl not only enjoyed it — at an age when none of them could do anything but run around the room on tiptoes pretending to be fairies — but wanted to stick with ballet when the exercises became more demanding. Then the teacher said she ought to do tap and modern and musical theatre and God knows what, but Storm's family could not afford those classes and instead of choosing from the many, it was easier to take none.

This is how the only artistic feature about Storm remained her given name. Storm? What could her parents have been thinking? Perhaps her mother just wanted to imitate the celebrities who came up with the most peculiar names for their offspring.

Storm did not shine at school, (actors largely don't, so the cliché goes), but soon showed interest in school plays and poetry readings. Her inspirational teacher suggested drama school for her, and she must have had something, because she was accepted at both the places where she auditioned. It was probably the last year when you could get a grant to a drama school, so she was able to take up the offer.

She was not conventionally pretty, but at drama school she had the opportunity to play absolutely everything from queens to servant girls; in fact, following the new gender-neutral trend, kings and butlers as well.

During the last year, her teachers predicted a good working path before her. But as the academic year's end was approaching, a cold chill moved into her bones. What if I can't get a job? How will I survive?

The final production was *The Cherry Orchard*, where she played Dunyasha, the maid, a smallish part. In earlier productions she had given her all: first, as Antigone; then, in an Ayckbourn comedy, where she was so funny, she stopped the show. But the outcome was absolutely nothing—no one seemed to want to represent her. Then having lost all hope, she went on as the maid and a well-known agent materialised and signed her up.

That was an early lesson in the discovery that you never have any idea what will be the project that propels you forward.

When college was finished, she stayed in her old digs and took a waitressing job to sustain herself, while her agent talked about lots of auditions soon. Lots?...In fact, precisely three television interviews came her way. She didn't get any of the parts. That was very disappointing. For each one she had to learn a long speech and perform it on camera.

She didn't even meet the directors of the plays, only the casting director. Nobody talked to her. After sitting outside on a chilly landing, she was called into a room and asked to deliver her speech to camera. At drama school it had been all about getting into the character. But now there was no time. Just get on with it. When she finished, they politely said goodbye. They didn't even bother to use the famous phrase 'We'll let you know'. But then everybody knows that they never do let you know nowadays—they call you only if they want you.

On the way out, after one of these castings, she bumped into a classmate from drama school. She'd always disliked this girl, and they were in very different gangs. Now they greeted each other with genuine affection. In this cold, alien environment, a familiar face was everything. They were in the same shoes, and Storm beamed a great good luck wish as she left the premises.

After three unsuccessful auditions over four months, Storm decided that it must be in the theatre where her talents lay. Her agent was a bit disappointed—after all, the quick buck was in television work where the benefits went beyond the money: once they knew a face from a television soap, it was much easier to get work elsewhere as well.

Storm had just about decided to take on more shifts at the restaurant (there seemed to be little point in keeping herself available for non-existing interviews), when her agent called: would she like to meet the artistic director of the Maidenford Theatre for a chat? They were planning their thirty-year anniversary season and wanted to make a bit of a buzz getting some well-established actors.

Maidenford...Maidenford...Where the bloody hell is that? thought Storm, while on the phone. But when she heard that they were considering her for the peach of a part, Sonia in *Uncle Vanya*, she suddenly didn't care where the place was — she would crawl there if she had to.

The first meeting with Michael, the artistic director, went well. It turned out he had seen two of Storm's final performances at the college and he'd asked to see her. So much for her agent saying that it was she who had suggested Storm for the part. Michael was completely bald, had an earring in one ear and talked in a very soft voice. Storm really had to strain to hear every word he said. After a bit of general chat, he said this was just an initial meeting, and asked Storm to come back next week and give an audition speech.

"Would you like to hear something classical or contemporary?" asked Storm.

I leave that to you. Any emotional link to Sonia, whispered Michael — or at least Storm thought that's what he'd whispered, as he'd said it so quietly.

She was in a state of flux. What speech to present? Something that she knew already? Or should she learn something new, closer to the character she was auditioning for? She prepared different pieces but couldn't decide until the last moment. Then she went with a contemporary but gutsy American play that had nothing to do with Chekhov.

It was probably the unsuitability that surprised Michael and the panel—the sheer audacity of it, and they gave her the part. They called her just two days after the audition and told her that Sonia was hers. "Yes!" And she punched the air. Not a bad start for my professional career!

She gave notice at her digs but worked at the restaurant right up to the day she was to take the train to Maidenford.

Evelyn

Six weeks before opening night

It was dark in Evelyn's room; the curtains were tightly drawn and only a narrow strip of light on the duvet betrayed the daylight outside. She could only sleep in the dark. But she was not asleep at the moment. She'd woken about twenty seconds ago, her heart racing. She felt slightly sick, and she had a general feeling of dread in her stomach. She sighed deeply. "It will pass." She was trying to calm herself as she gritted her teeth.

She had woken up like this most mornings for many months. She didn't need a particular reason to feel scared, it just happened. Then she had to think calmly about the forthcoming day and realise rationally that nothing was planned for the day that would alarm her. If anything, it was going to be another boring day in the life of an old pensioner.

But, of course, the old adage is that actors don't retire. Evelyn certainly had no intention of doing so, but sometimes circumstances force you to have a break. It is the same with being out of work. How dare non-actors call this 'resting'? How could you possibly rest if no money is coming in and your career is paused?

That was the other thing she noticed about herself: she was often angry. Sometimes, it was without any reason, or just for annoying trifles that would not have bothered her when she was younger.

Now, her first task was to calm down, steady her heartbeat and begin the day. A quick shower usually calmed her nerves and put her back on an even keel.

After showering, she pulled on an old tracksuit and tottered to the kitchen to fix some breakfast. She had lived alone for so long that she couldn't even imagine having another human being moving about the premises.

She was never lonely, though, because there was always the work. She had been very lucky in this precarious profession. She had had so many wonderful opportunities in the theatre, playing leading parts in many of the classics. She was a very young Ophelia, then became a member of the Royal Shakespeare Company. The part she had had most success in was Ranevskaya in the *Cherry Orchard*. What a fabulous part! When she made herself think of it, her anxiety subsided a bit.

It was not easy to keep working. The price was to be content with small, character roles, sometimes just a 'cough and a spit' as the minor roles were often referred to in the profession.

Many older actresses didn't or couldn't make this change. Sometimes, it is a bitter blow for an ex-leading lady to come on stage as the old nanny and shuffle off a few minutes later. But it was important for Evelyn to keep going. And, once she had the reputation of a reliable old actress, she was seldom out of work.

She was pleased to be offered the chance to go to Maidenford to play old Voynitskaya in *Uncle Vanya*; it was a change to play a sophisticated lady, and patter on in French. More than anything, she once more would enjoy the companionship of the theatre. Being part of a company, mixing with colleagues of all ages, kept her young and interested in everything.

She welcomed the news that the cast included Bella Foster — she was quite a name, and her return to the stage would be noted by the press. It was a mystery to Evelyn why it was that, at her age, success and visibility still mattered to her. After all, those articles and interviews would never mention her, but it was still important that she be part of something noteworthy.

There were some advantages being the oldest in the cast: the theatre fixed her up in a small hotel, rather than some dreary digs; she'd really grown out of those. Altogether she was really looking forward to the experience. In a week's time she would be in Maidenford for the read-through.

Uncle Vanya, here I come! she thought.

The Read-through

Bella spent a long time choosing her outfit for the read-through. This would be the first time the full company would meet; it was important that she'd make a good impression. She wanted something that would make her look younger, as she still fretted about the unfortunate gap between her own age and the character's she was going to play. At the same time, she didn't want to appear to be trying too hard — mutton, dressed as lamb.

She was careful not to show off either. After all, actors in provincial theatres were badly paid, and her wardrobe had a great deal of designer stuff that might be tactless to display. She was sure that being elegant was not on the menu at Maidenford Rep.

She decided on jeans (very ordinary but youthful) and a colourful silk blouse (showing some leading lady power). She made sure that she was not too early, so that she could make a bit of an entrance.

When she walked into the rehearsal room most of the cast and crew were already sitting at a long table; at the head the director, Michael, all in black with a mournful expression. My God! thought Bella, I wish we were doing a comedy — hoping this wasn't going to be one of those self-lacerating rehearsal periods when everyone had to 'reveal' themselves. She'd left those exercises behind in drama school.

She at once caught Evelyn's smiling face. Evelyn beckoned her. "Hello little one, come and sit here!" Now this was encouraging. Evelyn was less than twenty years her senior, but she was going to treat her as the young 'ingénue'. She took her seat next to her. The director rose and came to greet her, enwrapping her hand between his own and looking into her eyes, thus signalling he was really pleased. Not too bad, being back at work, thought Bella.

It was time to look round the table and register the others. The well-known actor who was playing Vanya waved languidly; they had worked together once in the distant past. Bella had just slipped her jacket off when she felt a hand on her shoulder. She turned round and faced a tall man who was holding out his hand. "Just like to introduce myself, I am Gabriel, I am playing Astrov." He got hold of her hand and kissed it lightly. She smiled and said hello, meanwhile thinking: Oh, I see the type, the smooth matinée idol who likes ladies. She recalled to mind some of her own acting romances — she was determined not to make those mistakes again.

Storm was busy talking to the stage management and other technical staff who were more her age and she felt comfortable with. She did not introduce herself to Bella.

Meantime, Evelyn continued chatting to Bella — how excited she was that they were working together—and was giving all the details of her uneventful train journey from London. Bella only heard half of it; she was nervous, and she wanted to take in all the new faces.

Michael, the director, started speaking. He had such a soft voice that everybody stopped chatting, straining to hear him. He introduced everybody and explained their function. Some people took notes to remember who was who.

The rehearsal room had no windows, and it was painted black. So was the theatre itself—just a black box. From this you were led to surmise that, here, serious work was undertaken.

Then they started to read the play. The famous actor was murmuring a bit, not giving anything away. It was not necessary for him to prove himself. Storm gave her all, and one could sense that she was going to be good in the part. A bit different from the usual wilting Sonias—a stronger, more modern version of the role.

Bella knew the text by heart. She had been too nervous to leave learning the words until the rehearsal period. Not that she wanted anybody to know this, so she pretended to read it. At the same time, she decided to use the occasion for establishing contact with her fellow actors. She looked up from the script a great deal and studied them with interest. She had learnt, long ago, that listening was probably more important than speaking at this early stage. When you speak, you say something you already know; when you listen, you learn something new.

She noticed that Gabriel was working the same way. Michael was pleased to see that there was already some sort of chemistry between his Astrov and Yelena.

Evelyn had few lines to say, and half of those were in French. Even though she was slightly worried about her French pronunciation, she figured that in present company no one would know better. She had plenty of time to watch the others. She knew it was vital for her to keep working, yet she often noticed that a slightly bitter taste gathered in her mouth on these occasions. She could not stop herself remembering the wonderful leading parts she'd played. She'd had outstanding notices in the *Cherry Orchard* in a production in Manchester. There was talk that it would come to London's West End but it never happened. In those days, she was the centre of attention. Now, while she could feel how the younger members of the cast were watching and weighing each other intently, she was largely ignored. She found it difficult to focus on the proceedings. These Chekhov characters were so miserable. It was fashionable to find the funny side of their situation but, fundamentally, they were all unhappy.

Her thoughts drifted to her own family. It was all ancient history; she'd divorced her husband a long time ago. Surely that was better than these unfortunate characters locked together in misery. Yet, there was the question of her only daughter. Why could they not maintain a decent mother and daughter relationship? She'd tried so many times but her daughter always resented her. She never knew the real reason; perhaps her ex-husband had succeeded in convincing the child that she was secondary to her mother's work and career. Who knows? For some reason, her daughter felt that Evelyn disapproved of her actions, her choice of jobs, her choice of partners. Anyway, it was too late now… Suddenly she heard the director saying, "And that is the end of Act I. You, Evelyn, remain on the stage and make some notes in your book. Oh dear, she thought to herself, I have so little to do, and when it is my turn, I am miles away. Luckily no one had noticed.

"Let's have a break, there is coffee in the Green Room," said Michael with a slightly less gloomy expression.

Bella decided to pay her respects to the 'Great Actor'. She walked up to a group surrounding Auberon; everybody was holding paper cups, and Bella could feel the collective admiration and amusement that was directed towards the late-middle-aged actor who was going to grace the Maidenford stage with his Vanya. Not only was Auberon a great actor, he had the reputation of being a charmer, kindness itself to fellow actors and an altogether delight to work with. Now, he was entertaining the group with his amusing theatrical stories of which he had many. He was also a great mischief maker, and the theatrical world was full of anecdotes about his practical jokes.

When he noticed Bella, he stopped in the middle of his story and turned to her immediately. "You're looking fabulous. More beautiful than ever." Bella nearly blushed, but then remembered that she was well beyond the age of blushing. The rest of the group politely shifted aside, leaving the two actors to chat.

"It seems as if it was in a different life when we worked together all those years ago," said Auberon.

"To be honest I am really surprised you remember," Bella whispered, with a somewhat faux-humble air. "I bet you don't remember where and in what it was," she continued.

"It was in Nottingham; it was in Private Lives by Coward and you played the small part of the French maid, who starts the play."

"I am amazed. I didn't think you ever noticed me."

"You had an awful French accent, and yet people remembered you and predicted a great future for you," he went on.

Bella laughed, covering up that no matter how pleased she was that Auberon remembered her, the French accent remark still stung.

"Yes, nowadays they would have a real French actress playing the part. As for you, I remember how the audience worshipped you. The queues waiting for you at the stage door were so long it was difficult to get past them after the performance."

"Ah well, my matinée idol days are long behind me," said Auberon with a chuckle, like somebody who is not regretting it for a second. "The roles get better for older men," he said.

"Maybe, but not for women," retorted Bella.

It was time to get back to the reading. Bella had a lovely warm feeling inside her, the kind you only get in the acting fraternity. Years can go by, but it all continues as before—decades can be breached in moments.

The second part of the reading went even better. Everyone was more relaxed, and the general feeling was that they couldn't wait to get down to work.

Blocking

Everybody was already at the rehearsal room, and stage management had marked up the set with tape on the floor. Instead of the proper stage furniture, various grotty substitute pieces were scattered around. It was a few minutes after 10, which was the starting time for the rehearsal, but there was no sign of Storm.

The director continued the small talk, didn't want to make everybody aware of the young girl's lateness. At ten minutes past, though, he felt they ought to do something, and announced that instead of the scene in the opening act when all the actors are on stage, they'd start with the night scene between Vanya and Yelena.

As they all busily turned pages in the script, Storm arrived out of breath.

"I am so sorry...I got on the wrong bus...I ended up on the wrong side of town...My God, not exactly scenic!" she was saying while peeling a very long scarf from her neck.

She was wearing a short and tight denim jacket, a skirt that could hardly be called a skirt—more like a strip of cloth over some orangey leggings—and a pair of heavy hiking boots, which finished her attire. They also seemed to finish Evelyn, who was muttering under her breath, "What on earth is she wearing?"

The elderly lady was dressed in navy from top to toe. She used to wear black all the time but now thought it too ageing and too Mediterranean, so had opted for navy, paired as always with a colourful silk scarf around her neck. She thought herself very *chic*. Not that anyone ever noticed.

Now that Storm was here, they could go back to the original rehearsal plan and start on act one, which meant shuffling pages of scripts again. Everyone was a little tense except Storm, the one who had arrived late.

Eventually rehearsal started.
Scenes when the whole cast is on stage are usually the most difficult to rehearse. First, the director 'blocks' the moves for the actors who then follow the directions slavishly. After all, they have little idea of their characters yet, and they are not in a position to argue.

Michael obviously had done his homework and he marshalled his troops with confidence. As they proceeded with the play, everybody made marks in their script, indicating where they were supposed to move to and when. Except Storm. Bella noticed immediately that she didn't write anything down; she'd be in trouble tomorrow, she thought with a tiny bit of glee. She won't remember where she is supposed to be.

Evelyn kindly asked: "Would you like a pencil dear? I have a spare one..." "No thanks," waved Storm. "That's fine."

Auberon's script was an amazing sight. He used several colours to mark up the lines, their meaning all very mysterious. But he had given many outstanding performances based on his rainbow scripts, so who was to argue with him?

Gabriel was very quiet, but his glances always followed Bella. Every time she looked up from the printed page, she noticed that Gabriel just happened to look at her. She was beginning to feel almost uncomfortable, but then she remembered that Gabriel's character, Astrov, is fascinated by Yelena, so she put the actor's glances down to his trying to establish the relationship with her character.

She herself was far from establishing what her Yelena would be like. The more she studied her part, the more she felt that this woman was boring. Yelena says so herself in the play. Now, how do you play somebody who is boring without your performance ending up as such?

When she'd been offered the part, she'd reacted to the thrill of going on stage again in such an iconic play and flattered that the company thought of her for such a young role. Yet that was the other problem—she could not overcome her anxiety that she was too old for the part. And, as if that was not enough, they'd cast an Astrov who was younger than the Chekhov character. She imagined Gabriel would put some white highlights in his hair for the performances. Of course, the dialogue in the play often depicted people who complain about the perils of old age in their forties, the truly ancient people supposedly being in their late sixties. Times have changed! It would not be right to be faithful to the original ages in the script.

Work went on, each individual actor fearing that they would make a fool of themselves. Well, maybe not all of them. Storm was so confident — you could see how she was enjoying the process of rehearsal. Not that the others had any reason to worry. Nobody was paying attention or was evaluating their fellow actors — they were so utterly occupied with themselves.

Auberon was busy making marks in his script. The others were sensing already that he was going to make an excellent Uncle Vanya. He had the talent of being charming to everyone and, at the same time, being utterly absorbed in his own self. Bella noticed that he was extra charming to the good-looking, young assistant stage manager girl, Amanda. This wouldn't be a surprise to anybody — they all knew of his reputation for preferring to socialise with the young.

At the end of the day, the general mood was good. They all felt they'd done a good day's work and they'd managed to get through the first half of the play: two whole scenes. If they could do the same the following day, they'd move on to working without scripts and taking every scene apart.

While Bella was putting her copy of the play into her smart handbag (she was the only one who didn't carry her stuff in a backpack) Gabriel came up to her.

"Do you think, we could run the lines together some time? I find it so much easier to learn them that way. Only if you don't mind, of course."

Bella turned around and looked at him. Thoughts were running through her head. Is this an invitation to something other than learning lines? Surely for her those days were over when colleagues made a pass at her. But she also experienced a tingle of excitement coursing through her veins, and, before any further thought, she said: "That would be great. We can both benefit from it."

The ASM, Amanda, who had overheard, interrupted enthusiastically: "I don't mind being on the book if it helps. I can help out whenever you want to meet." Bella felt a little disappointment. "That would be very kind of you. One day next week after rehearsal? Can we use this room, do you think?"
"I'll make sure I have the keys." All three of them looked pleased in anticipation. Of course, it is just running lines, nothing else, thought Bella to herself and skipped out of the room with light steps.

At the end of the rehearsal day, Evelyn felt really tired. It was a tiredness that only old people could feel. She used to get more tired, even exhausted when she was young, but after a little rest she would recover. Now the heavy limbs and the aching back would stay with her all the time. Especially after a day like today, when she'd worked about twenty minutes of the rehearsal day and spent the rest sitting on a chair waiting.

She liked watching the others work, but not for a whole day. She never complained though—she knew that this was the way the theatre worked, and she was grateful for the job. What would she do with herself otherwise?

She most certainly didn't want to retire and join the local pottery class, or something fashionable like a mindfulness course. Her mind was full enough, and she didn't want to learn how to empty it, or how to breathe properly. She was taught that in drama school.

She took her time gathering her clothes and bag, making sure she had everything, as nowadays she tended to leave things behind. She paid particular attention to putting her script away, with the notes she'd made during today's rehearsal. It would be mortifying to lose those. It was one of her regular nightmares that she had to go on stage but couldn't remember her lines, and her script was nowhere to be found.

She watched the rest of the cast leave; they all bid goodbye to her but none of them stopped for a chat. They all scattered hurriedly in the darkening evening light.

What are they hurrying for? she thought to herself. Here we are in this strange town. Nobody has family here. Nobody has mates in the pub waiting. Where are they all going? Perhaps they just didn't want to be stuck with her.

She slowly, but with a straight back, left the theatre, and made her way to the small hotel where she was staying. Calling the place a hotel was somewhat pretentious of the proprietors — it was more a medium-size boarding house. But at least she didn't have a landlady who imposed all sort of rules.

On the way home, she went into Tesco's to buy some cheese and a couple of apples for supper. That would do. She wasn't hungry at all. The breakfast was quite generous; she would have something cooked in the morning.

In her small room she put the television on and found only terrestrial channels available. On the BBC there was some ghastly quiz show, but she let it play for some company. She was soon in bed and felt better immediately. She thought of tomorrow's rehearsal and went to sleep in a good mood.

It was already dark when Storm finished her run. She tried to run at least three times a week. She had her special gear for it: lycra tights, shorts and a beleaguered T-shirt with holes in it. She always regarded runners with beautiful matching outfits as amateurs. If your running clothes looked pristine, you surely didn't run a lot.

It was time to return to her small, rented room. She remembered that she hadn't had any supper — perhaps she could get something at the 24-hour Tesco store. She was wearing a red bum bag with her purse inside; she stopped and looked to see how much cash she had. Not much. What was worse, this was all the money she had until the end of the month.

In truth she was in trouble with her finances. When she got this job, she had bills to settle, the rent for her notice period and her share in the utility bills. Plus she had to put down some money for her new accommodation, and of course the train fare. Now she'd found she wouldn't get paid until the end of the month. Basically, she was broke.

How to economise? Maybe, today, just get a banana and a yogurt. But she was really hungry.

Oh, to hell with it, she'd get a pizza. She'd have half of it and the other half would do for tomorrow.

Back at her digs, she crept into the kitchen, hoping not to meet her landlady. Tough luck — Mrs. Brown was at the sink doing the washing up.

"May I stick my pizza in the oven?" she asked.

"Sure, dearie, though I hope you won't eat this rubbish every day," the landlady remarked. "I've just finished my pork chop with two fresh vegetables. That was a proper meal."

I would prefer that as well, Storm was thinking, if only I could afford it.

Unfortunately, Mrs. Brown was in a chatty mood. "Do you know why I don't like to go on holiday?" she asked.

"Hmm?" Storm tried to make a genial sound, thinking, why would I want to know that?

"Well, if I don't do the washing up, my hands go all funny. My nails get grubby. It is not at all nice."

When the pizza was ready, Storm looked for a plate and asked if she could take it up to her room.

"You can if you want to, but aren't you more comfortable here?"

"I have some studying to do," lied Storm. "I'm really behind with learning my lines."

"Just as you like. You kids are always in a hurry. Looking at your telephone while eating is not very healthy, you know..."

She was still speaking when Storm was out of the kitchen, climbing the staircase in twos, to reach her room as quickly as possible.

Now that she'd reached it, she looked around and realised how uncomfortable and limited the space was. Where to put the plate? There was the bed, the bedside table and a chair, and that was it. She crouched on the bed, put the plate in front of her and ate half the pizza. She would take the other half back to the kitchen when the coast was clear.

She removed her running clothes and stretched on the bed in her bra and panties. Despite her surroundings, including the sad, cold, half pizza, the nylon bed sheets and the shocking pink bedspread, she felt happy and excited.

What a part Sonia was! Probably the best in the play. To land something like that as her first proper job after drama school...Holy Moley! And she felt that she was going to show them all!

And what a pleasure it was watching Gabriel working. It was going to be easy to act being hopelessly in love with Doctor Astrov. Gabriel was the type all women fell for. And she was unlikely to be the exception. This thought made her happy and excited. I will not fight it, she thought—it will probably add a great deal to my performance. In drama school, they'd impressed on her the necessity to gain life experience. She was ready to gain as much as possible.

Bella arrived at the theatre early. Over the last few days, her confidence had been fading in her ability to seize the part of Yelena. She must find something more in the character than the beautiful woman everybody wants. As far as she could see, Yelena has no appealing qualities. She is a drip, she thought to herself.

She calculated that if she arrived early, she might have a chance to speak to Michael — morose Michael, as the cast had started to call him behind his back. Indeed, the director was already there talking to the costume designer.

Bella sat down on a chair and tried to put on an expectant expression. Michael clocked it and, after a few minutes, finished his discussion and asked Bella if there was anything she would like to talk about.

It was not an easy conversation for her. She didn't want to reveal her anxiety but she wanted to share her concerns, and hoped to get some help in creating an intriguing woman.

She became concerned when Michael agreed that Yelena was the least interesting character in the play. Thank you, she thought, and how was this going to help me? But Michael went on to explain that the reason he cast Bella, was because she had such a special presence on stage. He also reminded her that it is not necessary to play beautiful. When you play a king, it is the reaction of the others that will make you majestic; and in this play, the same — it is other people who see Yelena as beautiful. No need to act it. Well, you can't, can you, thought Bella.

"Another thing," said Michael, "I notice you sometimes touch your neck when you are speaking. I like that. Yelena is suffocating. Use that," he added with a mournful expression.

Bella felt a bit better. She certainly wasn't going to share her concern that she was too old for the part. After all, very little could be done about that.

Towards the end of their conversation, the rest of the cast started to ooze in. Evelyn on time as usual, with her neat handbag which always contained some fresh vegetables, carrots or mushrooms for her to snack on. She peeled the mushrooms with slow attention, and had them raw. No wonder she was so stick-slim.

Bella had to fight her weight — always watching what she ate, always counting the calories. She had a small frame, and the extra kilos easily showed. I can't wait to be as old as Evelyn, when it won't matter anymore, she thought.

Evelyn slowly peeled off her navy cardigan, looked at Bella, cursing the years she had to carry and the aching limbs. If only she could be as young as Bella again.

Auberon sauntered in casually elegant as always, yet you could see already how he was going to transform into the untidy, shabby Vanya, whose unhappiness impacts on everybody in the play.

Gabriel and Storm came through the door together. Storm was carrying a coffee in a paper cup; Gabriel held the door for her. Bella looked up and felt a tiny prick of jealousy. How stupid; there was no reason. If Gabriel was interested in anybody, it was surely her, Bella. That, at least, is what she was reading in his glances.

Rehearsals went well — this middle period being easier. The first shock of meeting all the new people and facing a new environment was over, but they were still some way from the opening night and facing the audience. This was the time when you could experiment. Unfortunately, Bella was of the old school and not fond of experiments. She thought deeply about what she was going to do, and tried to achieve it in rehearsal.

She watched Storm, with envy, throwing herself into all sorts of unlikely situations with abandon. Bloody hell. She will act me off the stage, thought

Bella. She noticed that Michael loved the way Storm was working. Even when he said: "No Storm, I don't think this will work... but interesting, very interesting," there was admiration in his voice.

Well, of course, she has nothing to lose, thought Bella, with a touch of bitterness — all the time seeing the reviews of her Yelena in her mind's eye. 'Much loved leading lady from our TV screens fails to conquer the stage. Her languid performance hardly travels across the footlights'. Damn it, I won't be languid. I'll show them some grit!

While the others were working, Bella was thinking of the 'word rehearsal' they'd fixed with Gabriel for the evening.

They'd arranged to meet at the theatre at eight o'clock. There was no show on that evening; the theatre was dark. The atmosphere was so different from the daytime, or even from the evening, when there was a performance on. The dark theatre with a few working lights seemed forlorn, without a purpose.

Even though it was not an old theatre, it seemed to have ghosts. All the players who had trod on that stage were somehow present.

Bella went past the sleepy doorman, who must have been a replacement for the usual cheerful girl sitting there during the day. She introduced herself, but the laid-back young man didn't seem to be interested, just waved her on. Curious, the doormen always used to be old chaps, kind of old retainers, who nevertheless didn't recognise anybody and failed to pass on messages, thought Bella. Well, some things did improve with time. But not many.

Soon, the assistant stage manager turned up as well. Amanda was an overenthusiastic ASM—perhaps this was her first job. She laid out her script, several pencils and a giant eraser. She sat down expectantly, not quite sure what was going to happen.

Bella did not find small talk easy, and she felt nervous. This is ridiculous. Why am I nervous? she thought. I am the one who knows the text. I am only here doing a favour for a colleague.

Gabriel arrived late. He didn't apologise, though the whole rehearsal was his idea. To be fair, it was only five minutes or so, but it seemed more to Bella. The ASM had her nose in the script, unaware of the private drama playing out in Bella's head.

Gabriel threw his leather jacket on a chair and started rummaging in his canvas messenger bag for the script. He found it and placed it on the table. It was surprising what a bad state it was in, considering he claimed that he had just started to learn his lines.

"What would you like to do?" asked the ASM.

"Up to Gabriel," said Bella.

"Well, I'd love to go through all the scenes that we are in, even if it's not just the two of us on stage," said Gabriel turning to the girl. "And, Amanda, you can read all the other parts. There was a moment's silence, then he looked at Bella and added: "if that is all right with you."

Bella gave the girl the most charming smile, "Sure, whatever helps." Amanda was just pleased that he'd remembered her name. General goodwill all round.

They started working. It became apparent that Gabriel knew more than he'd let on. He was familiar with the text; only sometimes it wasn't exact. He was good at improvising, but the text was a new translation by a well-known dramatist, and it had to be syllable perfect.

They went through the crowd scenes, there being hardly any scene when they were on the stage by themselves. It turned out that Bella knew her lines but not the cues. Gabriel found this very amusing, and, like a conductor, waved Bella in when it was her turn to speak.

This could have been slightly insulting, but Gabriel did it with such charm that Bella had to laugh. In fact, she giggled like a schoolgirl. If anybody had been listening outside, they would have thought they were rehearsing some French farce.

When it came to the famous scene when, late at night, Astrov and Yelena are alone, the giggling stopped. Gabriel never took his gaze off her—clearly understanding the essence of the scene: that no matter what the dialogue was, the chemistry between them should be electric.

Bella was slightly embarrassed. It was only a word rehearsal; there was no need to play out the scene. But she didn't know whether it was the way Gabriel was working, or there was some kind of seduction going on. She found it difficult to forget herself in a scene that they had hardly rehearsed.

She glanced at the young ASM for some clue but she was looking at the text, following the lines with concentration. Can she be oblivious to what is going on here? she was thinking.

At the end of rehearsal, they were all tired and quite pleased with themselves. They had certainly made strides in learning the lines. Bella felt elated, feeling she would be able to make a success of this part. Although she didn't much like pubs, she thought they'd all earned a drink and suggested they all go to the corner pub near the theatre. But Gabriel excused himself and said maybe some other time. Bella was stuck with the girl.

Gabriel hurried away, while the two women walked to the pub. It was quite difficult for Bella to keep up a conversation while her thoughts were elsewhere.

Evelyn had the problem of what to do with her evenings in a provincial town. She even had some days off, as her part was quite small and she was not needed at all.

Having visited the cathedral, the local museum, and a National Trust property, she ran out of things to do. It worried her that, even with so little occupation, she was feeling tired and anxious all the time. Even on days when she didn't have to go into the theatre, she woke up with palpitating heartbeats and a fear of something unknown.

When she was fully awake and had a little talk with herself, she calmed down; but the tiredness remained. She must have a blood test soon, she thought. She didn't like going to the doctor, always joking that if they looked hard enough they'd be certain to find something wrong.

She quite liked going to the market in the town. She always picked up some fresh vegetables, and the fruit was also nicer than at the supermarket. Unfortunately, she didn't have any cooking facilities, but she always stopped to look at the butcher's and the fishmonger's stalls. She remembered those fun dinner parties she used to give. The guests were mostly actor colleagues or directors or designers she had been working with over her long career. They came to taste her famed cooking and have a fun time. She used to love cooking: it, too, is one of the creative arts, she'd always tell herself.

Nowadays, who would she invite? Half those friends and acquaintances were under six feet of earth, or their ashes scattered in bizarre locations. The ones who were alive had so many ailments and treatments that the conversation would become gloomy and lopsided. Quite simply, her world had shrunk and too many doors had closed.

She'd often thought that she was guilty of not having 'civilian' friends who had nothing to do with the theatre. In her younger days, she'd tried to enlarge her circle with neighbours and people from the local library. But when they asked her whether she was 'resting' — when she was miserably out of work — she realised that her efforts were in vain. How to explain that she was not a 'luvvie', and she'd never rested in her life, but was waiting for opportunities? And how could she explain that she did not want to retire? She'd rather sit on the night train, go round the country, and stay in shabby little hotels than sit at home comfortably in front of the telly, knitting.

The world of actors was simply different.

She counted herself lucky to have opportunities to work with some regularity and intended to go on until she dropped off her perch. That is why she never mentioned her palpitations and anxiety to anyone. It was important that they saw her as somebody who was reliable and healthy. She was known as an old actress who still had her marbles, could learn the text, and deliver it the way it was required of her. God forbid that somebody would spot her weaknesses and stresses. She wouldn't last another day in the profession.

Latterly, she'd had less free time as the rehearsals had progressed. The actors were called every day, and she had the opportunity to watch the others rehearsing. She liked this company. They were all accomplished, talented actors, doing the work they loved best. As she watched them, occasionally, just a few times, she felt bitterness that she was watching from the wings, instead of playing those weighty parts herself. She had to remind herself that she was an old lady now; those roles wouldn't suit her.

But in her mind's eye, she was eternally young.

Work in Progress

After a few weeks' rehearsal, everybody had learnt their lines. Without the script in hand, the serious work could begin.

Storm enjoyed rehearsing. She was one of those lucky young actors who had few inhibitions. She was happy to try anything; if the director wanted her to deliver her lines standing on her head, she would do it without questioning it. She was not intimidated working with the 'great actor', and their scenes together were going especially well. The two of them had become the core of the play, as if it were about Uncle Vanya and Sonia, and the others were just visitors in their world.

No matter how much Storm liked rehearsing, she would always arrive at the last moment. The older actors would all be present when she'd come in, hurried but not even slightly embarrassed by the fact that she was the last. She'd throw down her backpack, which had seen better days—she'd owned it since her middle school days—and unfurl her long scarf, while the others looked on, some wondering whether she might have an Isadora Duncan moment, and strangle herself with it.

Morose Michael pretended to be busy, so it wouldn't look like the whole company was waiting for

Storm. When she started working, everybody instantly forgave her. There was so much freshness, so much truth in her delivery that it was obvious they were in the presence of some outstanding talent. The whole company knew that although people outside the profession often imagined that actors are jealous of talent and are bitchy and competitive, nothing could be further from the truth. If the person you are acting with is very good, you will look better too—you just have to raise your game.

Even Bella enjoyed watching Storm rehearse, forgetting that she had worries about her own role. Sonia, compared to Yelena, was a better part and Bella envied the freedom with which Storm flavoured each line.

Gabriel watched Storm even more intently than the others. He had a slightly disconcerting gaze that one could imagine might disturb women and put out a signal that he was interested in them. Storm noticed it, but contrary to what she thought and even hoped for a little, Gabriel never approached her in breaks or tried to chat to her more than was necessary when among colleagues.

At lunch breaks, Storm always found a quiet corner when she gave herself over to her phone. It was difficult to imagine that she had quite so much business to attend to; in fact she was busy—trawling through social media sites.

She wasn't happy with her accommodation, and was looking for somewhere less expensive, and without a bored landlady who watched her like a hawk. She was now searching the student sites and was looking for a flat share. After all, she wasn't so far from her student days.

Today was her lucky day. There was a room advertised not far from the theatre; no deposit was needed because the previous person had just left the flat, dropping out from university. This suited Storm who was always broke. She made a call straight away, and the thin little voice at the other end said the place was still available, but she must come this afternoon because there were lots of enquiries.

Storm didn't hesitate for a minute. She went to Michael and asked for the afternoon off for personal reasons.

Everybody was a bit stunned; they were of the generation that believed that the show must go on. Unless you were dying, and Storm obviously wasn't, the theatre came first. But there was no way of knowing what kind of dire emergency she was in, so nobody made any remark.

When she left, Michael released everybody except Gabriel and Bella.

"This is a good chance to work on the night scenes, when you two are alone," he said.

The characters' first encounter wasn't a long scene, but it was the moment when it becomes clear that these two are attracted to each other. How far they will go in revealing their attraction was what they had to decide today.

They started off with Yelena's long monologue, when she admits to herself that she can't wait to see Doctor Astrov and spend time with him. As always with Chekhov, the characters say one thing but feel something quite different. Yelena promises Sonia, who is in love with Astrov, that she will sound out the doctor to find out how he feels about Sonia. It is obvious that Yelena only takes this task on because she wants to be alone with Astrov and talk about something intimate.

After the monologue, Astrov appears and the two are alone for a while. Again, Astrov talks about his plans for the forests he owns, but he admits that the reason he visits every day is because of Yelena.

Gabriel put the map of the forest on a table and Bella instinctively drew near him. She placed her hands on the map, and for a moment she had a sharp view of her own hand there. It was the hand of an older woman. Suddenly she could not disguise her age. On the table she saw her mother's hand, and she was ashamed of it. She could not withdraw it, because

Yelena would not have done so. But Bella wished she could hide her hands.

Gabriel noticed nothing of this. He was getting more and more heated, as Astrov admits his love for Yelena. Gabriel was one of the few actors who could enact a passionate love scene and seem sincere. There are some great actors who are uncomfortable playing such scenes. Bella had met quite a number of them in television. No matter how ardently they looked at her, she could see that there was nothing behind the eyes — it was all sham. Not Gabriel.

He was on fire, and when he took Bella in his arms and kissed her according to the script, Bella felt an enquiring, tasting tongue in her mouth. She kissed him back, and there the scene ended. Vanya was supposed to enter, but Auberon was not there this afternoon.

They both stood hot, slightly breathless with burning cheeks, and suddenly embarrassed, returning to their own selves. Bella was taken aback; it was unusual to go for a full passionate kiss in the rehearsal room. Especially, nowadays, when many actresses would object to such vehemence. Should she say anything? Should Gabriel have asked for permission?

But she remained silent. Michael was nodding and murmuring, "Good work, the scene is at a good place. It will be terrific."

Yes, thought Bella this is going to be terrific.

"Please Bella, go up to wardrobe; they are waiting for you for a fitting," said Michael. "We're finishing early today to give you time."

Gabriel gathered his bag and walked up to Bella. "Goodbye, my angel," he said and gave her a light hug.

"See you tomorrow," whispered Bella as if it was for an assignation, and not for the next day's rehearsal.

At the wardrobe fitting, the costume designer remarked, "None of your earlier measurements are right. Are you losing weight?"

"Could be the cuisine of Maidenford," said Bella, rather pleased.

Secretly, she knew that the weight loss was due to that knot she'd been feeling in her stomach, ever since she'd first glanced at Gabriel.

The Accommodation

Eventually, Storm found the advertised accommodation in a small cul-de-sac. Compact terraced houses, once workers' cottages, lined the narrow street; most of them were poorly maintained. She looked for number 23. When she got there she found the front door open and loud music pouring out onto the street. This must be it, thought Storm.

A skinny girl was just removing her Wellington boots in the narrow hallway, which was covered with anoraks, trainers and assorted scarves, half hanging, half on the floor.

"Come in," said the girl and Storm immediately recognised the thin, babyish voice she'd been talking to on the phone. "Let's go upstairs. The room is on the second floor."

Goodness, there is a second floor, thought Storm — these houses looked so small from the outside.

They climbed to the top of the house up a steep and narrow stairway; the second floor was a loft conversion. Surprisingly, the room looked quite spacious, maybe because the only furniture in it was a mattress on the floor. Then Storm noticed, also on the floor, a small cage and in it two white furry animals.

"What are those?" asked Storm.

"Oh, they are pet mice, they are very sweet," squeaked the girl.

"What are they doing here?"

"They belonged to the previous tenant. She promised to come back for them, but, to be honest with you, I don't think that is going to happen."

"What shall we do with them?"

"I think we should keep them a bit longer, in case she does come back."

"Cool. And...where is the bathroom?" Storm enquired while thinking about what the hell to do with the mice.

"It is one floor down; I'll show you. It is a bit of a mess now, but we have a strict rota for the cleaning, so normally it is ok."

Storm put her head around the bathroom door and, having seen the state of the shower curtain, decided not to investigate further.

"I'll take it. When can I move in?"

"Whenever you want."

"Well, it is the end of the week, so I can move in tomorrow."

"Do you have a lot of furniture?"

"I have nothing." When Storm saw that the girl arched her eyebrows, she added quickly "I will have to buy a few essentials."

"Cool, I will tell James who collects the rent that you will pay tomorrow," said skinny and turned on her heals.

"No problem," said Storm to the wall.

But there was a problem. She had no money at all, and the next salary was not due until the end of the following week. She'd had no credit card since she'd got into money trouble during her student days, and decided not to be tempted by the lure of the plastic. The good news was that, with this move, she'd be reducing her rent by almost half.

The following morning at the theatre, tactfully, nobody asked Storm how her 'emergency' went. She was desperately thinking how she could get hold of some money by the end of the day. Who could she borrow at least a hundred pounds from for the rent, and to live till the end of next week? First, who would have money to spare? Gabriel...definitely no. Auberon...definitely yes, but she could never sum up enough courage to ask the great actor. Surely Bella would have spare cash, but she was so grand it would be humiliating to ask her. That left Evelyn. The older generation was always preaching how not to live above one's means. Surely Evelyn would have a little stack tucked away. On the other hand, Storm felt that Evelyn was the only person who disapproved of her. Her clothes, her manners, her opinions. Still, it had to be her.

In the first coffee break Storm sat down next to Evelyn who was munching on a biscuit she'd brought in her magical, all-containing bag.

"I would like to ask you a big favour," started Storm.

"What could that be?" asked Evelyn surprised.

"It is really embarrassing, but I am in money trouble. I have to pay my rent tonight in my new digs, and I have precisely three pounds thirty in my pocket. Any chance I could borrow a hundred pounds from you till salary day?" she blurted out in one go.

Evelyn was taken aback. "Oh, my dear girl, oh dear..." she said, and then paused. Storm's heart was beating hard. It was a mistake, I've made a mistake, she thought.

After a few seconds Evelyn smiled and sweetly said "I don't have that much money on me, but after rehearsal, if you like, we can go to a cashpoint and I will give you the money. You know I wouldn't even ask for it back, only I myself try to live on a tight budget."

"Oh, no question, you will have it back end of next week. Thank you so much, you are a star," said Storm and hugged Evelyn passionately.

To Evelyn's surprise, she felt her eyes welling up. "Oh, go on. I think Michael wants you for the next scene." She gently pushed Storm and turned away. I must be a complete idiot, she thought to herself, but strangely, she had a warm, pleasant feeling spreading in her stomach. She even forgot her aching limbs.

Having packed her few possessions, Storm appeared in the student house with her rent in cash and moved in officially. She was calculating that she could even buy a small table and a clothes rail at the flea market, if she was careful with her hundred quid.

Then she might even ask Gabriel to come and visit her, and they could discuss their scenes together and talk about their relationship in the play. Yes, that might work very well.

There were only ten days to go before the opening night.

During the final week of rehearsal, a strange request came from Gabriel. He asked for Bella's advice. After his latest divorce, he was living in a rented apartment on the edge of the town, and he felt it was time to buy a property before all his savings melted into nothing. He'd got to like the countryside around Maidenford. The position was good and central, and London and the Midlands were within easy reach. Obviously, property around here was much cheaper than anything near London. He had already seen a cottage he liked, and wanted Bella to look at it.

"We could go after rehearsal. It is about a twenty-minute drive out to the country," said Gabriel, and gave his irresistible begging look.

Bella hesitated for a second; this was odd. Did Gabriel really want property advice from her? What did she know about property? Or did he just want a companion for his evening drive? He could have asked any of his male colleagues in the cast to go with him. Why did he choose her?

She didn't want to think about the obvious implications, yet she felt compelled to say yes. It would make a lovely change after the stressful rehearsals to get out into the fresh air and think about something other than *Uncle Vanya*.

"We'll go straight after rehearsal. My car is parked in the free parking about five minutes' walk from here," he said.

"Jolly good. I think I'll be able to walk that far," said Bella. "Just about."

After this conversation, Bella found it difficult to concentrate on the work. She went through the scenes mechanically, but her mind was elsewhere. Could Gabriel be making a pass at her? Had he guessed how she felt about him? No, that couldn't be. She'd been careful not to show anything that was not entirely professional, even in the love scene. Although that deep kiss at the end of the scene had confused her, she'd told herself that Gabriel was an instinctive actor and he was just carried away by the moment.

But this? It can only mean that he is smitten too, and wants to spend some time with her away from the theatre. Yet, she must not fall for him. She was fifteen years older than Gabriel — she would make herself ridiculous. 'Mature leading lady falls for handsome rascal actor'. She could see the headlines.

Somehow the working day came to an end, and the cast were gathering their stuff to leave the theatre. Bella put on her short jacket over her jeans, tied her scarf and discreetly sauntered over to Gabriel.

"Here you are. Ready? Then let's go!" he announced at the top of his voice. So much for making an inconspicuous exit.

They walked to the car, which was much further than Gabriel had implied, but Bella didn't feel tired. She felt free, and took great big gulps of fresh air.

They got into the car; Gabriel had to shift a lot of his clothes from the passenger seat.
"Do you always carry your full wardrobe with you?" asked Bella teasingly.
"I've been meaning to take these inside for days, but something urgent always happens."
"Urgent? What?"

"You know, life interferes."

"Aha..." she had no idea what he meant, except that his life seemed to be very messy, like his car.

They'd left the town now, and were driving in pretty countryside. Even though it was late autumn, the colours were still stunning. The sun was setting and all the foliage had a golden glow. It was just the right setting for their play in rural Russia.

"It is the first time I've been outside Maidenford. I didn't know how lovely the countryside was around here. Always just rush to the station to catch the train. From station, straight to the theatre, and that's it," said Bella.

"I hate the train. I'd rather drive, even if it takes longer. I feel I am in control."

"You like to be in control, don't you?"

"What is that supposed to mean?"

"Just that. You don't like people telling you what to do."

"That's unfair. Don't I take direction well? Do I argue with the director?"

"I didn't mean it professionally. I am guessing in real life."

"Ah, real life. Where does real life begin and professional life end? Yes, you are guessing. You know me little."

"I would like to know you better," said Bella and immediately regretted it. This could sound like an invitation to dance.

"So tell me about the cottage we are going to see," she said, quickly changing the subject.

"It is in the middle of this small village. It has three bedrooms and a large garden. I mean it is not really large but proportionate for a cottage."
"Sounds lovely, away from it all."
"Yes," said Gabriel sounding very sincere, "I am not an urban person, I am much happier in the country."

Then they both became quiet and that was nice. You have to be comfortable with somebody to keep silent.

After a half hour drive, they arrived at a village; it seemed to have only one street. Gabriel turned into a narrow driveway, just a dirt road, and at the end of it he stopped the car.

"Here we are," he said.
"Where is the cottage?" Bella asked.
"It is behind this fence," said Gabriel, walking up to a small gate.
Bella followed, even though her thin pumps were not the right shoes for a country outing. It was dusk by then, and the cottage could not be seen at all.

Gabriel tried the gate but there was a big padlock with a chain on it.

"I can't believe it – this gate has always been open. I knew nobody would be in the house, but I thought we could see it from the outside."

Bella looked at the hedge and the locked gate. Somehow, she didn't mind that they'd come for nothing. She started laughing.

"This is no joke – we will have to climb the fence," said Gabriel.
"What? You must be kidding, I can't climb through there," she said, alarmed.
"Course you can, my angel. I'll give you a leg up."

Before Bella could take the next breath, Gabriel lifted her up and placed her on a large log. He pushed her from behind while she got her legs over the wooden fence. She arrived on the other side with a bump but no lasting damage. Thank God for those early ballet classes, she thought.

Gabriel scaled the fence easily. With his long legs he hardly touched the edge.

They were able to walk up to the cottage, and indeed it was charming. They peered in through the dirty window and could see a lovely old stone fireplace in a low-ceilinged room. Through the back door they could spy the kitchen, which was very basic. "This has to be updated, but I could do it myself. I am pretty good at DIY."

"Are you planning to retire?" asked Bella. "You want to move to the end of civilisation and then spend months doing up the house? Don't you want to carry on with acting?"

"Of course I do. I can do both. This is not that far — if I have to go somewhere I'll take the train from the nearest station."

"How far is that"?

"Oh nothing, thirty miles."

"You are crazy. What if you are snowed in?"

There was a pause and Gabriel looked troubled.

"Don't you like it, then?" he asked.

"I like it very much. I am just trying to be practical, since you asked me."

But Bella wasn't feeling practical. There was an incredible gaiety inside her as she reflected on climbing a fence in the now pitch-black garden and giving advice on a most impractical property. She must have been a teenager when she'd last climbed a fence. It was all ridiculous. Wonderfully so.

Then, as she was trying to climb back, Gabriel held her very close. She could feel his heartbeat through his leather jacket. It was a clear night, and a starry sky completed the clichéd romantic scene, and Bella felt she knew what the next step would be. Her face was close to Gabriel's. She felt his breath on her cheeks.

But the moment passed, and Gabriel safely deposited her on the ground, and asked anxiously "So you don't think I should put in an offer?"

Bella pulled herself together. "It is charming, but you really have to think about it, how practical is it, for you?" Bloody hell, I sound like my mother, she thought.

On the way back, they chatted about the production and gossiped about the others. Bella looked at the young man in the dark and saw in his occasional glance that those dark eyes were just as caressing as before. They got back to Maidenford, and Gabriel drove her to her door.

"Thank you for coming with me. You really are a mate," he said.
"It was a pleasure, I had a great time, but you know what—don't buy that cottage until you get married."
"Haha, that'll be the day. I have no intention of doing that again."

"It was fun having an outing, thank you," said Bella cheerfully, forgetting for a few seconds that being a 'mate' of Gabriel wasn't exactly what she was aspiring to.

Only a week to go

In the neat guesthouse, where Evelyn was staying, it was always quiet. Evelyn hardly met anyone on the stairs or at breakfast. The businessmen had to leave earlier; Evelyn was always the last in the small breakfast-room, as rehearsals usually started at ten, and the theatre was only a ten-minute walk away.

Evelyn cherished that walk; she took small, brisk steps and inhaled great gulps of fresh air. She always set out early and regarded it as her daily exercise. She took it seriously.

But this morning was different. A curious thing had happened to her. When she'd woken up, she couldn't remember where she was. She looked round in the small room and everything seemed strange and unknown to her: the single bed with a white bedside table; the red curtains with heavy fringes; even her own clothes, folded neatly on a chair next to her bed.

Her heart started pumping, and in her panic the more she wanted to remember the less she could make sense of her situation. I must have had a stroke, she thought, and the dreadful thought was strangling her throat. The first thing she could remember was that she was in a play. But what was the play? And where was she? What were her lines in that play? She could not remember.

That was the most upsetting thing. She knew clearly that she was an actress. She also knew that if she could not remember her lines that would be the end of her working days.

She carefully started to move her hands, then her arms, then her legs. Everything worked fine. Maybe it is not a stroke then. It must be something else. She must see a doctor. She washed and dressed with shaky hands and, by the time she was ready, it had become clear to her that she was in a hotel. She went downstairs, luckily found somebody at the usually unattended desk and asked the lady if she knew a doctor in the vicinity she could see.

The middle-aged lady at the desk had a kind face, and showed concern about Evelyn's well-being.

"I hope nothing serious. Maybe, if it is urgent, you should go to A & E," she said, putting her glasses on. She gleaned from Evelyn's expression that she was not keen on the idea. "Actually, there is a walk-in clinic not too far from here; it is only three stops on the bus. Here, I'll write down the address for you. Have you had breakfast?"

"Oh yes, I will have breakfast now," Evelyn said, wanting to reclaim her normal routine. She was hesitating for a moment about which way to turn for the breakfast room, but the lady at the desk pointed

73

towards a door. "Look they are still serving, the lights are on."

Evelyn turned towards the door and entered. Slowly the room and the objects around her seemed more familiar. But still no clue what town she might be in or what the play was she was rehearsing. Suddenly another panic gripped her—what time was she supposed to be at the theatre?

She had her breakfast and afterwards asked the lady at the desk if she could kindly call the theatre and say that she was delayed. She figured there would be only one theatre, and they would know in the hotel why she was in town. Indeed, the lady said, "Don't worry, I'll call them. You just go and see a doctor."

Evelyn took her coat, and clutching the piece of paper with the address of the clinic, left the hotel. She had the bus number written down, and after a few minutes it duly came along.

At the clinic reception they asked her name and permanent address, and she was relieved to realise that she could answer it all. She explained what had happened to her in the morning, and maybe because she was at a medical establishment, she felt more confident, and slowly her memory began to return. She remembered what play she was in, and immediately wanted to say some of her lines quietly, but still nothing came back. The dread returned.

When the young Asian doctor called her, she was able to recall her whole morning experience quite clearly. The first thing the doctor did was to check her blood pressure. "This kind of memory problem often comes from a surge of high blood pressure," he said, reassuringly. "Do you have your blood pressure checked regularly?" he asked. Evelyn had to confess sheepishly that she normally didn't bother with such things. Her blood pressure was quite high, but not alarmingly so.

By the time the doctor had finished all the procedures, Evelyn found that she could remember everything. "So how long would you say the whole episode lasted?" asked the doctor.

"I suppose about an hour...an hour and a half," she said in a better mood, but still anxious.

"I am going to give you some tablets to keep your blood pressure down, and you should have a scan just to make sure that nothing nasty is going on inside your brain. Are you staying in town for a while?"

"Yes, I am in the production of *Uncle Vanya* at the theatre," she said proudly, and with great relief.

"You will get an appointment from the hospital for a MRI brain scan, but don't worry — it could be just one of those things," said the doctor, not looking up, just filling in papers and making notes on his computer.

It was a relief to know where she was and what she was doing. But she still felt a suffocating anxiety about her state of health. Work was everything to her. She couldn't remember when she'd made the decision that work came before family. In fact, she'd never made such a decision; often it is circumstances that make decisions for you.

It all started with her divorce. Never marry another actor, she could hear older colleagues warning her, when she was a young actress. That is easier said than done. Who else was she likely to meet, be in a work situation with, get to know, other than members of her profession? Oh yes, a director would be a fine thing! But in any production there is only one director, and lots of actors.

So, despite all the warnings, she did marry an actor. She was playing Lavinia in *Mourning Becomes Electra,* and he was playing her brother, Orin. Eugene O'Neil's play is about incest, and they played it to the hilt. On and off stage. It was inconceivable that after the production had finished they would be apart. Within two months they were married in an intimate ceremony in a register office. Only a few friends and hardly any family, as they would have had to travel from distant places.

She remembered the day with great affection. Evelyn could never understand the need for lavish weddings that were in fashion nowadays. People getting themselves into debt for what? Her daughter, Amelia, had one of those weddings and possibly was still paying back the money she'd borrowed, but Evelyn wasn't there. She wasn't invited. By then she was divorced from Amelia's father, and her daughter blamed her for the split. She had easily got over the divorce, but her daughter's behaviour pained her every single day.

Why was she blamed for something that she was not responsible for? It proved to be true that two actors can seldom maintain a good relationship — career comes between them. While Evelyn was offered work constantly, mostly in the theatre, which involved being away from home, her husband struggled to stay in the profession. He spent more time at home and got closer to Amelia.

Maybe that was the reason why the grown-up daughter blamed Evelyn for 'never being there'. But who paid the rent? Who bought the clothes she was wearing? Who paid for the occasional holidays? This was not considered by Amelia.

Evelyn's thoughts were overwhelming in her buzzing mind. Maybe, after amnesia, comes the rebooting of memory. It was not even she who'd left the marital home. Amelia was away in college when one day, after a tour, Evelyn went home, and her husband was gone. Amelia never forgave her. Is this fair? — she had been asking herself a thousand times since. Is it fair that she was never allowed to see her grandchild?

These were the wounds that never healed for Evelyn, and that is why work was everything for her. If she could not go on working, her life would be truly pointless. She had to get on with the here and now and concentrate on the job.

As she was leaving the surgery, she remembered that her rehearsal call wasn't until 12 o'clock today. She took the bus and set out for the theatre. It was only half past eleven — she wouldn't be late after all.

As the days passed, the individuals were forged into a company. Within a couple of weeks all these strangers had one goal: create a good production, maybe invent something new within the constraint of an old well-known play. They became a unit, a squad, in military terms, with a common aim.

Bella, as the leading lady of the company, felt a desire to make the bonding stronger and decided to organise a party. The venue was going to be Gabriel's flat, as it was obvious that some members of the company didn't have two pennies to rub together; and the *chef de cuisine* was going to be Bella. She had a signature dish that she always made for her dinner guests, and she was going to repeat the feat: a chicken casserole, with Eastern spices and some fruit. You could make it in great quantity, and just serve it with fresh bread.

They chose a humble Tuesday, because at the end of the week people tended to disappear. The full company of actors was invited, plus Michael and the two stage managers—eleven souls, as Yelena would say in the play. Bella had her work cut out, but her enthusiasm was boundless.

When Evelyn heard about the party, she wondered who in the company was having a fling? In her experience, when parties were organised in a company, it usually meant that some people wanted to spend more time together outside their working hours. She didn't have a candidate for sure, but suspected that Bella and Gabriel might fit the bill. Nevertheless, she was grateful for the distraction and offered to help. Bella said it was all under control, and declined. Some people offered to bring a bottle, which was accepted.

On the day, early in the morning before rehearsal, Bella went to the market and purchased all the ingredients. In the theatre green room there was a fridge; she crammed everything in there. After the day's work, Bella and Gabriel rushed to the apartment, and Bella started cooking. It was quite a challenge. Gabriel's kitchen equipment was somewhat limited, to put it mildly, but Bella was on fire. She was cooking in three different pots simultaneously, and she made the place festive with paperchains, tablecloths, and plates.

Everybody arrived almost at the same time—these theatre actors were a disciplined lot for keeping time—and the dish was soon served with French bread, which was Auberon's contribution. Gabriel provided the soundtrack through his laptop computer. The wine flowed, and everyone praised Bella for her effort as well as her cooking.

When the food was gone, Storm stood up and started dancing. Amanda, the assistant stage manager, joined in immediately. They were not dancing together, just enjoying the rhythmic movement. Michael surprised everybody with his moves—he was obviously a serious disco goer; and when the lanky stage manager displayed the same aptitude, contorting his long limbs into fancy shapes, there could be no doubt that these two fellows attended the same sort of venues.

The surprise came when Auberon set sail, leaving his regal armchair, the only such furniture in the flat. Not wanting to dance alone, he took hold of Storm. This involved a bit of 'dad dancing' but somehow it looked right for Auberon. Just as in his acting, he could get away with anything.

Perhaps Gabriel was a fan of Latin-American music, because a tango number suddenly brought a change of atmosphere. Auberon took up his tango position with Storm and, as they tried perfecting the sultry style, Auberon's hand brushed over Storm's breast once or maybe twice. She barely noticed, and when the number came to an end they finished with a flourish. In the general rowdy applause, Storm thought nothing of the rogue hand of Auberon.

Evelyn was watching all this with pleasant nostalgia. She was full of lovely memories, dances of the past, other companies, other cities. She'd noticed earlier how Bella and Gabriel looked at each other. It made her remember an ardent actor who wanted to seduce her, the young innocent of the company, and said to her "Do you know what Maxine Audley used to say?" (Who would remember now the flame-haired actress? mused Evelyn.) The actor continued:
"She said that on tour it is not a sin."

I still didn't give in to him. The thought amused her. Rejuvenated by the memory, Evelyn got to her feet and joined the dancers. The company couldn't believe their eyes. She was still a good mover, and though her dancing didn't last long, they could see that, once upon a time, this old white-haired lady must have been quite a 'hot chick'.

Meanwhile, Bella was in the kitchen with Gabriel. How different this kitchen was from her spic-and-span designer space at home, yet she had never felt more contented than at present. Gabriel was also caught up in the atmosphere. He took Bella in his arms, their smiling faces were close, and at that moment the most

81

natural move for Bella was to kiss him on the lips. Gabriel returned the kiss and, for a while, they were forged together like a bronze statue. When they parted, there was a strange expression on Gabriel's face, his eyebrows knitted, his eyes questioning: Is this what you want? It was just a fleeting moment, but Bella was slightly taken aback by that look. Surely her kiss could not be a surprise? When they re-joined the others, the dancing was over and a sultry jazz number was under way.

The party was winding down. Uber cars were ordered. Bella felt as if, instead of blood, champagne was coursing through her veins. Gabriel's curious look had just been a momentary distraction. She was about to offer to help Gabriel clear up, when the lanky stage manager asked her would she like to share his car…they would be passing her hotel anyway.

There was a moment's silence—it seemed to Bella that everybody was looking at her. She made the only decision that was possible to maintain her decorum…she accepted the car-share offer. She tried to catch Gabriel's eyes, but he was in a deep hug with Auberon.

As Bella was gathering her things together, everybody present burst into applause to thank her for organising the party and cooking a delicious meal. She made a light curtsy and waved to everybody on exiting. There will be other nights…there must be, she was thinking.

In Costume for the First Time

The whole cast was gathering on stage in various state of undress. In theory, they should all have been dressed in their costumes, but almost everybody had some quibble about the finished product. The director and the costume designer sat in the auditorium muttering to each other and talking to the cast on stage.

"We'll look at everybody one by one, and when we've finished, will you please leave the stage? When we are through, we are going to start the run of the play," came the instruction from Michael.

They started with the smaller parts and eventually got to the leads. Vanya's costume was fine, except it looked a bit too new. They all agreed that Auberon had such an elevated look that he needed to be 'broken-down' a bit, to give the right impression for the dishevelled Vanya.

"No problem, we'll put some dirt on the trousers and put the jacket through the washing machine a few times," said the designer. "Acting might help a bit," murmured Auberon, under his nose.

They decided Storm looked perfect in her simple pinafore dress and blouse; she only had the one costume and a shawl for the whole play. There was a bit of talk about her hairstyle: she wanted to keep her short hair without plaits or extensions, but the 'creatives' argued that it would be wrong for the period. Eventually they all agreed that a simple hair extension gathered in a low ponytail would do instead of the plaits.

It was Gabriel's turn to be inspected when Bella arrived on the scene. Everybody stopped talking as they gazed at her in silence. She looked stunning. Maybe, because of her yellow dress, it seemed as if someone had turned on the lights.

"Oh my, you do look beautiful!" exclaimed Gabriel, "If you come on like this I think I'll have to leave the stage—no point trying to act with a vision like this."

Everybody laughed politely, but Michael was not happy. "She cannot wear this huge hat. You can see nothing of her face!"

"And we know that the punters have paid a lot to see precisely that," said Gabriel. Only he could get away with a joke like that, referring to Bella's television past. She let the remark pass and her eyes were searching for Gabriel's approval. As far as she could tell, Gabriel was really impressed. "The yellow works like a dream. Who knew?" he whispered to her.

Both director and designer got so excited by Bella's appearance and her hat-size that they forgot Gabriel standing centre stage waiting for judgement. But he just stood there patiently.

Eventually they sorted out Bella to everyone's satisfaction, and she left the stage to change into her second outfit.

Gabriel's clothes were approved, except he'd have a smaller overcoat; the one he was wearing made his tall frame enormous like a Russian bear. A shorter, lighter coat must be found for him. He should wear his own donkey jacket for the rehearsal. With this everyone left the stage and the first dress rehearsal could begin.

Evelyn stayed in the wings during all the rigmarole; there were no problems with her black dress and small black headpiece, made of black tulle. It seemed to her that nowadays she wore the same costume for all her roles. Maybe she could bring her own, as in the old repertory days, when actors had to provide a set of clothes to fit various plays. Just vary the headdress. Silly old thing, she thought, be grateful to be in work at your age. But for how long? She could not get rid of the anxiety about her forthcoming hospital scan. It was time for the run-through. Full concentration ahead.

The dress rehearsal went well; there were only a few mishaps. The actor playing the professor, Bella's husband, knocked her hat off, thereby proving that the hat was too large and impractical. The actor was mortified. He usually played negative characters, as was the case here—everybody dislikes the professor. As happens so often, he was the sweetest, kindest man in real life.

Another casualty of the dress rehearsal was the dear old lady playing the nurse who tried to exit, and her shawl got hooked on the door handle, so she was stranded. They all laughed but knew that this is what dress rehearsals were for.

When it was all finished, Bella had to go to wardrobe to make a few adjustments to her costume and try on some hats. The seamstress, who was making the alterations, looked at Bella with admiration: "You look really fantastic in these clothes." "I am quite pleased, thank you," she said, and gave her most charming smile.

In a good mood, she was leaving by the stage door, when she saw that Gabriel and Storm were ahead of her on the pavement. Gabriel had his arm round the young girl's shoulders and they were laughing at some shared joke. Bella caught her breath. This is silly, she said to herself; two colleagues are leaving the theatre after an exhausting but satisfying day's work. But her good mood had evaporated. How stupid—what was I expecting from him? Absolutely nothing. And that is exactly what I got, said the voice in her head. Who the hell wanted a sordid affair in a rep company anyway, which could only end in tears? Could that person be me? She had no answer.

Storm and Gabriel were in buoyant mood. The dress rehearsal had given them confidence that this production was going to work.

Storm had noticed that during her last scene with Auberon, when she made her final speech, Gabriel had been watching in the wings. She'd found a new way into the meaning of these final words — which are often delivered in wilting, sad tones — about Sonia and Uncle Vanya being doomed to carry on with their drudging lives, and having "to work and work..."
Suddenly, Storm's delivery had taken on an anger, as in: "Why the bloody hell do we have to go on like this?" ... and everybody who was nearby sat up and listened.

When they'd finished, Gabriel had gone up to her, "You will be a terrific Sonia. No, you are a terrific Sonia." This was the first time he'd said anything personal to her.

"Don't speak too soon, I am superstitious. We have a long way to go before we open."

"Not that long, it is next week," he said.

"Yes, and it was obvious from day one that you will be a terrific Astrov," she said, paying back the compliment.

"From day one! That might be a bit of exaggeration," said Gabriel with his most heart-warming smile. "Maybe the end of the first week?"

"No, I knew it from the read-through, you can sense these things," she said with a very serious face, not returning his smile.

"Do you fancy a pizza after we have taken off this clobber?" asked Gabriel, "I am really hungry." Storm couldn't believe she was being asked out by Gabriel — it was always Bella he was eyeing. Something must have happened; up till now he'd seemed to ignore her.

"I'd love to but I am completely broke, so I'd better go home and eat what I have in the fridge," she said quickly.

"Nonsense, I'm inviting you for a pizza. Not exactly an overgenerous offer. I think we both deserve a little treat after today's good work."

Storm didn't hesitate anymore. "That would be really nice, thank you."

The evening was a success. Gabriel had a great appetite; he finished his huge pizza, and even had some garlic bread with it. Storm, who was vegetarian, had her smaller pizza and some tap water. They mainly talked about the play, and then they became conspiratorial, working their way through the cast, and gossiping about everybody. Gabriel was a great mimic and gave a hilarious demonstration of his skill. His Auberon was the best, capturing the haughtiness, mixed with a great desire to hear any gossip about anybody while pretending to be barely interested. Storm nearly choked on her pizza — it was so funny.

"What do your friends call you?" asked Gabriel. They can't call you Storm all the time, it's so severe. And your family, your mum?"

"I won't tell you, it's too silly."

"Go on, I'll keep it a secret."

"Ok, my mum calls me Zozo."

"Zozo, why?"

"I have no idea. I think I couldn't pronounce Storm."

"Better than Soso, or it could be Saucy!"

"You see, I didn't want to tell you."

Storm was embarrassed.

They were last to leave the place and Gabriel offered to take Storm home in his car. When they got to her house, in the student district, Storm was swallowing hard not knowing what the next step was.

"I am shattered, ready for the sack, I think we'll both sleep well tonight."

With this, he planted a light kiss on the girl's cheek and opened the car door. As Storm was sliding out of the car seat, something slithered to the pavement. Storm reached for the beautiful silk scarf. She held it up with a questioning expression. "When do you wear this, darling?"

"Oh, Bella must have left it in the car. I'll give it to her tomorrow. Funny, she didn't mention it," said Gabriel.

"She has so many, she didn't miss it." Storm risked a remark between her teeth.

"I've had such a lovely evening, my little Zozo. Sleep well – you deserve it."

The following day was Auberon's birthday. He invited everyone after work to the pub. Storm was looking forward to it. Suddenly she loved every single member of the team.

Bella was walking back to her hotel and her mind was buzzing. She was trying to figure out Gabriel's behaviour. It niggled her. Why did Gabriel spend so much time with her? Why did he single her out during and after rehearsals to talk to? And that first deep kiss that he gave her at the first rehearsal. She could see some in the company suspected that she and Gabriel were having an affair. Utterly stupid! As in the past, if she was having an affair with somebody, she'd make sure that no one knew. How unfortunate that there was nothing going on, yet people had started gossiping!

Once more she totted up the years in her head, the age difference between her and Gabriel. Fifteen years, yes, that is too much. She must not make herself ridiculous. Maybe he just sees her as the most interesting person in the cast. Or maybe he is just interested in the recipe for achieving fame on television. No, that was a horrible thought; she dismissed it immediately.

Yet, seeing him with his arms around Storm aroused in her the unmistakable feeling of jealousy; it was seeping into her veins. If I am jealous does that mean that I am in love? Or am I 'in lust'? No, no that couldn't be it; whenever she wanted to be with a man it was a yearning to love wholeheartedly, not just for sex. All she knew was that when Gabriel looked at her, her stomach contracted, her heartbeat quickened. It was enough to hear his voice on the corridor through the closed dressing room door: "Is Bella in already, is she in her dressing-room?" and she was melting inside, hearing her name spoken by him. Yet she never considered that it was love. She thought she had grown out of that sort of girlish infatuation — listening for someone's voice, feeling his presence in the room even when not looking at him.

Suddenly she hated everything in Maidenford: the role of Yelena, the cast in the play, the doom-laden director and, most of all, the hotel where she was staying. She wanted to go home.

It was a sudden decision. If she went to the station now she could be home in Kensington by ten o'clock. Her call wasn't until eleven thirty the following day and with the early morning train she could be back at the theatre in time. She had an overwhelming desire to sleep in her own bed and be surrounded by her own things.

She didn't need to take anything; all she needed would be there in her house. With a strong purpose she grabbed her handbag and marched towards the station. She was lucky – the fast train to London was leaving in twenty minutes.

Once on the train, the hurt she felt when leaving the theatre subsided. She had a purpose: she would check her post; she might even get a few more dresses – after all she hadn't taken anything smart for the opening night. She had just the right dress in mind. That should floor Gabriel. Oh no, she did not want to think about him.

In her charming mews house everything was in perfect order. Only one light was on in her husband's study. She quietly went up the stairs and opened his door. He had papers in front of him, his glasses were askew and he seemed to be dozing. At the sound of the door opening he looked up and smiled at Bella. "Hello dearest, aren't you asleep yet?"

Bella laughed. "Hello Theodor, I'm just back from Maidenford—I fancied a night in my own bed. I think you must have fallen asleep."

"Oh yes, silly me, for a moment I forgot where you were supposed to be. How is it going? I hope all is well."

"All is well, I just needed a little grounding." She hugged him and they both felt the warmth of familiarity.

"Shall we have breakfast together," he asked "as a treat?"

I am afraid I have to leave very early, you will be asleep," said Bella with real regret.

They agreed that he would come for the Press Night by which time the show should be in good shape.

After half an hour in her usual surroundings she calmed down and felt a lot better. It had been a good idea to come home. In the guest bathroom some lovely photographs of her were on the wall and two of her television awards were also on a shelf there. Guests often questioned why she displayed her awards in the toilet but she always said it was not a sign of self-deprecation, it was because people had more time to admire them in private. Anyway, for once, she herself paused for a minute to look at them. No use pretending—they made her feel good.

She woke early in the morning, opened the windows and breathed in the late autumn fresh air. She was a morning person; she usually woke up refreshed and with a positive attitude. Maybe that was the reason that films and television suited her better than the theatre. Some of her colleagues were true night owls. They were a sad sight in the make-up room in the morning but maintained that they were absolutely sparkling in the evening at the theatre.

Bella packed a small suitcase; in her *secretaire* she'd found some lovely cards that would do for good luck wishes for the first night and, miraculously, she felt excited about going back to the theatre. Before she walked through the door she looked in to her husband's room and kissed him lightly on his forehead. He smiled and turned to his other side.

She ordered a taxi to the train station. On the train she replayed in her head the scene in front of the stage door when she saw Gabriel and Storm departing together. In the morning light there was nothing in it. Nothing had happened—she was foolish yesterday—and now she was ready to go into battle on every front.

The run-through of the play started at eleven thirty. Before that some technical issues had to be sorted out.

Evelyn was making her face up in the mirror of the dressing room. It was getting more and more difficult to apply her eye make-up because when she took off her glasses she could hardly see anything. She was grateful that she did not use false eyelashes anymore. When she was younger they were part of her stage make-up; she was so used to them she could glue them on with a swish of the hand. Since then they'd gone in and out of fashion, but she didn't use them anymore. The mascara was enough trouble.

She put her small magnifying mirror down and stared into the large mirror. The face looking back at her was so strange; she saw an old lady, not unpleasant-looking but—oh so old and full of wrinkles! It was not an unfamiliar face but just wasn't hers. As she looked closer the reflection came into focus and there was the young Evelyn looking at her. She smiled—could it be a mocking smile? Old Evelyn was cheered by seeing this phantom—large blue eyes, undulating blonde curls—and she wondered which role young Evelyn was preparing for. The image was so clear that old Evelyn didn't want it to fade. It filled her soul with contentment. But it was time to go. Did she see young Evelyn raise a hand and wave?

The stage and the lighting were ready and the cast were called to the stage. First, they had notes from

Michael. On the whole, he said, he was pleased with everybody—there were only small refinements needed.

Bella waited cautiously; she knew from experience that small 'refinements' could actually upset her performance. It is a delicate business, the giving and getting of notes from a director this late in the game. But in this case the adjustments were mainly technical: don't mask so-and-so in the crowd scene; exit quicker after a scene; etc, etc. Evelyn was a bit disappointed—she didn't have a single note. Was she simply perfect or was her presence inconsequential to the production?

The run went well, though it felt a bit flat, just going through the motions. "We are ready. What we need is an audience now," said Michael.

After rehearsal they all went to the pub. It was full but the theatre group found a corner where they gathered to drink to Auberon's health. He was in a buoyant mood; it was one of those occasions when everybody loved everybody. Generally, this goodwill-to-all didn't last more than until the next rehearsal but in that pub they all thought they were the greatest bunch of actors and creatives that had the good luck to find themselves together. Typically, such feelings would surface again in the award season, when the recipient would mention how special their team had been.

Everybody respected Auberon. They admired not only his talent but his people skills. He was kind to everybody and was the ideal sort of man to lead a company. He was also a renowned teacher — he gave private drama classes and he discovered quite a number of promising would-be actors. His enthusiasm for young talent was the talk of the profession. Casting directors would listen to him if and when he suggested some youngster.

He always wore colourful scarves and the company presented him with yet a new one in striking colours. The wearer had to have a strong personality to get away with it. Auberon had it in oodles.

Bella had a bit of a cold. She felt her throat was hurting, and the men in the cast suggested a sure-fire remedy — port and brandy. Bella was not a great drinker but accepted the advice, and the drink not only made her throat better but resulted in a glow all over her body. Gabriel came and sat down next to her. His eyes were also a bit brighter than usual. They were teasing each other and laughing; anybody could see that there was something going on between those two.

Evelyn was watching them from a distance. Suddenly she had a very heavy heart. It didn't seem so long ago when it was she who had these flirtations in theatre companies; it wasn't so long ago when she was desired and complimented. When did she become invisible? As a young actress they often praised her beauty and she knew about the effect she had on men. She thought it was the most natural thing. Then, she did not think about the people who were born unattractive or were overweight, who never knew the feeling of being admired. Yet now, she was in the exact same position, she'd joined their league. No one would give her a second look. It was not easy to accept.

Between Bella and Gabriel the talk was obviously mostly about the theatre. The première was only days away and for the first time they were beginning to think about what would happen after this production. Gabriel wanted to know if Bella's agent was coming to the opening night.

"I am not sure, but I think he is planning to come," said Bella. "What about yours?"

"Mine is such a scoundrel; he always promises to come but something always crops up at the last minute to prevent him. I don't think he can be bothered to venture outside the M25."

"That's a shame. He should really see you in this."

"Thank you, my treasure." Gabriel smiled and kissed Bella's hand.

At that moment Auberon arrived with another port and brandy and placed it in front of Bella.

"Oh, what a happy couple! Here is more medicine; we cannot afford to have our leading lady be poorly.

By tomorrow you have to be cured!" And with that Auberon swished his new scarf around his neck.

By now, Evelyn was talking to Storm but was very much aware that the girl's attention was elsewhere. Evelyn enjoyed these gatherings but she always felt that most of her colleagues would rather be chatting to someone else. She had to stop thinking of the past and to accept that times had changed.

Her thoughts were interrupted when the others announced that they were going to have a game of darts. It was really time for her to go—she wasn't much good at drinking either. She slowly gathered her things and made her excuses to Storm, who seemed quite relieved that their chat had come to an end. She left the pub unnoticed by most of the others.

Bella had never played darts in her life, but, with two stiff drinks inside her and the encouragement of the men, she decided to have a go. At her first turn she wasn't sure what she was doing but her score wasn't bad at all. In fact, it was quite high. Beginner's luck, she thought.

Storm was quite good at the game and obviously extremely competitive. She would not have minded losing to the guys but certainly wanted to be better than Bella. Then a miracle happened, Bella hit the bull's eye and two double twenties and was the clear winner. The men were laughing; it was really amusing that Bella should beat them at their own game. "Stay on the brandy!" they shouted, "Told you it works miracles." Storm felt angry with herself—she should have been the one to beat the boys, not precious Bella.

Bella felt quite light-headed but knew it was time to quit while she was ahead. She looked for Gabriel; she still felt that kiss on her hand. Maybe tonight was the night—she had no resistance left in her, she would give in to him. Perhaps she might even initiate the first move. But she couldn't see Gabriel anywhere, then discovered him deep in conversation with Michael in a corner. Michael, in his black garb, had nearly disappeared in the dark but from his expression it was obvious they were discussing something frightfully deep.

Bella didn't care if she was about to interrupt a world-saving conversation—she did not want to disappear without saying good-bye.

"I am off now," she said looking at Gabriel, "I need my beauty sleep."

Gabriel looked up and his eyes connected with Bella's gaze. "Don't look at me like this," he whispered tenderly. Bella waited for a moment, feeling an overwhelming desire and great promise for the future, but Gabriel turned to Michael: "Say goodnight to our fabulous prima donna and darts champion."

Bella wished good night to both and left the pub. Her hotel was near; she needed the air. She went with light steps, her sore throat forgotten. She could only think of Gabriel's eyes when he'd said, "Don't look at me like this." The silly little sentence begged the question—why shouldn't I look at you like that? Are you afraid of me?

Early in the morning, three days before opening night, Storm had a phone call from her agent. She'd managed to get an audition for Storm with a famous American film director for a part in a blockbuster movie. They were looking for a strong young actress and wanted an unknown face. The director had already seen Storm's showreel tape, really liked it and now he wanted a personal meeting. The agent sounded excited, not an occurrence that Storm had experienced before.

"You know that I have an opening night in three days; how exactly am I supposed to appear in London?" said Storm, dismissing the idea altogether.

"My dear, this is a career-making opportunity, you cannot possibly miss this chance. I tell you, it wasn't easy to fix this meeting,"

"But I cannot ask for time off at this stage of the production. I would not have the courage to approach the director, it is unprofessional."

Her agent couldn't believe her ears. She was giving a once-in-a-lifetime chance to this young actress and not only doesn't she show any gratitude but she is also downright refusing the idea. How could she possibly think that her little production in the provinces was more important than this opportunity? Her agent was aware that it wouldn't be easy but the fact that Storm didn't show any inclination to try to attend the audition infuriated her.

Storm could feel the icy wind coming through her mobile, so she started to soften the conversation.

"I could try to ask Michael but really, I think it is hopeless at this stage."

"Well, you should try at least." The agent was also backpedalling somewhat.

There was a long pause on the line. It was just beginning to sink in, for Storm, what was at stake. She was totally committed to what she was doing in the theatre and, at first, she could not entertain even for a moment interrupting that work. But she was not stupid. This type of film was an opportunity that every young actress was dreaming of. Suddenly she felt unhappy and bitter. Of course, I will not be able to go to London, so now everything is ruined. I will not be able to enjoy the play and I will miss my opportunity to be in a film.

"What time do you have to be in the theatre?" the agent was asking.

"The run-through starts at ten thirty. Tomorrow will be at the same time, the exact time you are asking me to be at the audition. I don't know what it is I am asking? Could I see the director of the film after the opening night?"

"I am afraid not, he is flying back that evening."

"It is hopeless" sighed Storm.

"If you could come down tonight after rehearsal, I'll try to fix an 8 o'clock morning meeting, these Americans are early risers, but I won't do it until I am sure you'd be there."

"OK I'll see what I can do. Let you know." And then as an afterthought, "Could you at least send an email to my director here to describe the situation?"

"Will do." The agent's voice was cut off sharply.

Storm was staring at her mobile. Had this conversation really happened? She felt thoroughly miserable. It felt as if somebody had given her some tragic news, yet she should have been elated that such an exciting chance had arisen.

Bloody unfair, she was thinking as she got her things together to leave for the theatre.

For once she arrived early; she wanted to catch Michael before they started working. She walked upstairs to the office where she was hoping to find him. All the way to the theatre she had rehearsed her request and whichever way she turned it round it seemed more and more unreasonable. She just wanted the whole thing over. She would make her case, he would refuse it and then everybody could get on with the work in hand. And yet...missing such an opportunity so early in her career...Storm had a heavy heart.

When she knocked on the office door there was no answer. She tried again and this time a secretary opened the door and whispered: "They are all in a meeting, there are some technical problems; can I help you? The young secretary was rather breathless as if she was the one who had to solve all those technical problems."

"I need to see Michael for a minute," said Storm, losing the will to live at that moment.

"Well, I don't know, couldn't it wait till after rehearsal?"

"No," said Storm, surprising herself, "it is very urgent."

The secretary turned and went inside the inner sanctum through the padded door, which had the sign Artistic Director on it. Padded for the lunatics, Storm was thinking, which side of the door are they?

She stood waiting in the airless office, wishing she'd never come. To her surprise Michael appeared at the door, bleary eyed and shirt sleeves turned up, and before Storm could open her mouth, he said:

"I got the email this morning; it is an audacious request."

Storm wanted to say: So it is, forget it, I am out of here. But Michael miraculously continued speaking:

"As it happens we have a problem with the technical sound board. The experts can only come to repair it tomorrow morning, so we'll have to postpone the start of the run-through. If you can guarantee you'll be back by midday, latest half past twelve, you can have your morning meeting."

He'd half turned away when he noticed that Storm was just standing there without being able to say anything. Michael looked back over his shoulder and added: "Good luck, it sounds like a good opportunity – if you want that sort of thing."

Storm murmured a thank you and flew out of the room. She couldn't believe that the world had conspired on her behalf to be able to attend this appointment. Her heart was racing and she swore – I'm going to give a hell of a performance at today's rehearsal. And she did.

After rehearsal she had no time to go back to her digs, she just ran for the train. She got the ticket on her credit card – miraculously it was not maxed out. Anyway, her agent had promised they would reimburse her for the train fare. She got into the carriage feeling so buoyant she wondered how she would sit on her bottom quietly for the next two and a half hours. She wanted to shout to the world "I am going for an audition with a world-famous director tomorrow and I've just come off stage playing a peach of a part and I am marvellous in it. Beat that!"

She was not sure where she was going to spend the night. She didn't want to tell her mother about the interview—surely that would jinx it. She called a drama school friend, but she couldn't get through to her, and left her a message. She might have to spend the night on a park bench. Even that couldn't lower her spirit. Whatever is coming it will be an adventure!

She tried to read but, despite liking the book by a new Irish writer everybody was talking about, the words did not get through to her brain. She looked at the pages her agent had sent her—they added up to five lines of dialogue, which she had to learn. She knew them after two readings, so there was no point looking at them anymore. These types of action films didn't have much dialogue. She wondered whether they would make her do any physical stunts. Not her forte so far, she fretted.

Eventually, the train pulled into Paddington. She tried to call her friend again. Still no answer. Damn it, where was she going to spend the night? Ex-boyfriend came to mind; she was trying to decide between two awkward choices, mother or Mattie? Hmmm... She chose Mattie.

He answered from some very noisy place, sounding surprised. "Aren't you in Maidenford? I thought you were about to open."

Storm explained her situation and that she needed a bed for the night. Secretly she was quite pleased that Mattie knew about the play and even kept an eye on the opening night.

"Anyway, where are you, obviously in a pub having a night on the tiles?"

"I wouldn't say that, I am actually working. My shift doesn't finish until 11."

There was a pause, Storm was thinking, I should not have called him, it was a bad idea, he must be weighing up how to answer the request.

After a while Mattie said; "You know I don't have a spare bed, but if you are desperate of course we can share."

Storm looked at the time on her phone. It was past ten o'clock. She really couldn't ring her mum, she would have a heart attack or would spend the night scolding her. In that order. It just wasn't worth it. It had to be Mattie.

"Right, are you still sharing at the same flat?"

"No, I am sharing with my girlfriend," came the answer.

"Oh shit," thought Storm. "Well listen, that is awkward, forget it…"

"No," Mattie interrupted, "she is away actually, you can come, it will be fine."

"I am sorry, this is not good for you," she hesitated.

"It's fine, I have to go. Come to the King's Arms—you know the pub where we celebrated Johnny's birthday. See you soon." He hung up.

It was decided and she had no other options. She should have fixed it during the day but with the run-through and rushing for the train she had no time. Strictly speaking, she could have made time but she'd been sure she could stay with her girlfriend.

When she arrived at the pub there were quite a few people there still. Mattie was serving behind the bar and Storm had to catch her breath. Hell, he still looked far too handsome! Maybe this wasn't a good idea to ask him for a night's shelter.

He noticed her straight away and waved; when she reached the bar, they just high fived—it seemed more laid-back than a hug. She realised that there wouldn't be much conversation until his shift had finished. Just as well.

Storm was surprised to realise that she still had feelings for him. All through drama school, when they were together, the general view had been that Storm had won the lottery! Mattie was the hero of the class, playing all the romantic leads, while she was the plain Jane playing the character roles. Then, towards the end of the last year something happened. Suddenly, Storm started to shine, getting the opportunities for better and better roles. Then, at about the same time, Mattie was thrown out of his digs and he suggested they rent a place together.

By then Storm knew that the relationship wouldn't work. She'd had to listen for hours, with Mattie lining up his future projects. He was going to adapt a novel into a screenplay for himself to star in. He would direct a play on the fringe — he was in talks with the venue already. He'd had enough of the drama school's teachers, they were all useless; he would set up master classes and he himself teach at the Actors Centre.

These projects never lasted more than a few weeks. Then it would become clear that he'd only got half way reading the novel he wanted to adapt, that he hadn't found the play yet that he planned to direct, and the Actors Centre had never heard of him, let alone set up classes for him to teach. All in all, he was a fantasist in his professional plans as well as in everyday life. The charm of the golden boy faded and slowly the teachers and directors at the school could see that he was unreliable.

But as Storm was watching him pulling the pints she could still sense the charisma and her heart fluttered. Maybe she was judging him too harshly when she had told him that she did not want to move in with him. That was the beginning of the end. When

Storm secured an agent for herself (rather, the agent had agreed to represent her) and Mattie didn't even get answers to his begging letters, the relationship was over. They drifted apart without any dramatic farewell scene; it just happened. Storm had even texted him to say she'd got Sonia in *Uncle Vanya* and he'd texted back—Well done, you will be great.

And now she was dead tired, longing to go to bed and, instead, she was sitting in this pub waiting for closing time. After what seemed like an eternity Mattie was through, his shift finished, and they could leave.

Luckily his flat was not far away. His room was not unlike the accommodation that Storm had in Maidenford, but it was surprisingly tidy. Mattie could detect some appreciation on Storm's part: "My girlfriend, Maggie, is a bit OCD, so we keep everything minimal and pristine."

"She wouldn't be too pleased to see me here then, I don't fit in with the décor," said Storm attempting to introduce some humour into the proceedings.

But Mattie looked serious. "No she wouldn't be."

There was just one moment of electric connection gripping them both but Storm broke it.

"Listen I am really beat, I must get some sleep, I am supposed to be at the Grosvenor House Hotel at eight in the morning."

"Are you sure? I just thought maybe for old times' sake..."

"No, let's get to bed; I mean individually. Where would you like me to sleep?"

"As you can see it's a very large double bed so pick your side."

"You are a pal, you've saved me from an awkward situ, — did you say the bathroom was at the end of the corridor?"

Storm disappeared clutching her backpack and soon returned to the room in her pyjamas.

"I can't believe you still have these horrendous pyjamas," said Mattie, but Storm was already curled up in a ball and half asleep. Her thoughts were on her audition only a few hours away. Thank God, they won't be hiring me for my beauty...was her last thought.

In the morning Storm tiptoed to the bathroom and tried to refresh herself as best she could. She'd brought a pretty blouse in her backpack, a bit worse for wear now, and she was wearing her lucky jeans, the ones she had on for her *Uncle Vanya* audition. She went through her lines once more looking in the bathroom mirror and wondered what these lines meant. It was some science fiction speak she couldn't quite understand but hoped to make convincing nevertheless. She tried to remember her drama training, looking for some meaning behind the silly lines. She could detect none.

When she returned to the room Mattie was still fast asleep. She took a moment to look at him; he was sleeping like a cherub on a painting, long eyelashes and gently curling locks. For a moment she regretted that they hadn't slept together last night. But it was for only a fleeting second, then she remembered their history and she certainly was not in need of that. Complications!

She left a note, the torn off bottom part of her audition script with a 'Big Thank You, you are a star!' On the tube she felt unexpectedly nervous. This was the worst bit, travelling to an audition and to such a posh hotel too! She would have preferred the dingy rooms that casting directors usually inhabited.

At the hotel reception there was an assistant with a clipboard whose easy task was to spot the bewildered auditionees and escort them to a suite. Some people were already waiting, actors to audition and various unidentified persons with papers and clipboards. You could tell this was a big project where they would be spending a lot of money even before they'd shot a single scene.

Storm felt lucky to find a chair in the tumult. She was desperately trying to work out who had what function or who could be up for the same part as she was. But failed to come to any conclusion.

Then a girl was called whose face was vaguely familiar. Storm knew her from television; yes, she did quite a lot on the small screen, on top of which she was really pretty. Obviously, she was going to get the role, thought Storm. Why would they ever hire me if they can get her?

The minutes were dragging slowly but she didn't think of the train she had to catch, she was completely focused on the audition. At last, they called her name. She entered into a smartly furnished large room, with opulent curtains. Three people were sitting in armchairs and a camera was set up in front of them. The camera was angled on a chair. How could they find such plain and uncomfortable-looking furniture in this elegant hotel? — the thought flashed through Storm's mind.

Naturally, she was asked to sit on this chair. She looked at the three individuals facing her. In the centre was a middle-aged man with a perma-tan—she guessed he must be the director. He didn't speak. On his left a tense and pale woman sat. She was the first to address her. Storm supposed, from the British accent, she was the casting director.

"Hello, Storm, we are going to ask you to say the lines you received into camera; are you ready?"

Storm swallowed hard. No introduction, not a few polite exchanges of small talk. This was different from the theatre world. "Yes, I am ready," she said.

She decided to deliver the lines very dramatically as if it were in the middle of a crisis. First very softly, then with rising panic in her voice.

The director smiled. "That was interesting, completely wrong for the scene but interesting. I can see you are a very good actress."

"Really, how the hell would you know from this?" thought Storm but she smiled sweetly. "Of course, I haven't seen the screenplay, so I was just guessing the general tense atmosphere," she said.

"Could you try the lines now with great authority? You are frightened of nothing, you are giving orders; this girl will be a role model in the picture. Let's go once more."

Storm did her best to radiate authority, guessing wildly what 'role-model' acting was like, though she still didn't quite know what she was saying. By the end she'd become quite relaxed and ready to go on with the audition.

At this point the casting director said: "Thank you, that was very good, we will be in touch."

Storm sat there for a moment not believing that that was it, the big audition that was set up, involving so many people. She picked up her bag and left the room. At the door it occurred to her that she never knew who the third person was sitting there—they'd never bothered to introduce themselves. As she was leaving she noticed even more people waiting in the room outside.

Strom had absolutely no idea how her audition had gone. Not a clue. Did the director like her? Was she in with a chance? The whole thing was like a short nightmare. Except she'd known her lines and had said them. Now the rest was not up to her. She suddenly felt relieved it was over and thought of *Uncle Vanya* and the theatre waiting for her. She felt elated as she ran for her train.

PART TWO

Opening Night

The play has not started yet, but Bella is waiting in the wings. She can hear the buzz coming from the auditorium; suddenly she is like a racehorse. The twelve years she has not been on stage dissolve and she has that intoxicating feeling that soon she will be in front of a live audience. She is equally scared and delighted. The time for an audience has come. You can only go so far in rehearsals before you need people in their seats.

Her heart is pumping as if it wanted to jump out of the restricting corset, but Bella hopes that once she is on stage her fear will melt.

Gabriel passes her and squeezes her hand; he is taking tiny, short breaths. Bella is pleased to see that he is nervous too. They look into each other's eyes and both feel comforted. No words necessary. Gabriel walks on; he is on stage when the play opens.

The lights go up, it all begins. Bella can see Auberon in the wings at the other side of the stage. He blows her a kiss, which she returns.

In a few minutes she will be on. She takes slow, deep breaths. Storm is standing next to her. They will make their entrance together with some others — they are supposed to be returning from a garden walk.

Storm seems to have no nerves. More likely, she is just better at hiding them. But no, Bella observes, there is only keenness in her eyes, she wants to be on that stage in the limelight.

Storm is observing Bella as if she's conducting a scientific experiment. She can see that Bella is tense — her false eyelashes are trembling. Strange, thinks Storm, why do these people go on acting if it causes them such upheaval? Maybe they should call a halt. For Storm it is pure joy waiting in the wings to conquer the people in the auditorium; she can't wait.

Then they hear their cue and they are off. Bella draws a last deep breath, and she enters, leading the others in her yellow dress and matching hat to stun them all.

A few minutes later Evelyn makes her entrance. She makes sure that the book she is holding doesn't tremble in her hands. She is carrying an elegant silver headed stick, but it's been decided this is just an affectation of the character and not needed to help her walk. Her first scene is the wordiest; if she gets over it without hiccups the rest will be a breeze. She takes her place by the table, grabbing her book and cane. At this minute she only has one wish: I have a small role, let me not spoil it for everybody else, just let me get through it.

The opening scenes are a bit hesitant, everybody being careful to avoid mistakes. But, slowly, they all relax, and the play takes over.

Auberon is almost unrecognisable as Uncle Vanya. The exuberant, self-assured charmer seems a broken man. Without any help from make-up he looks at least ten years older. Unhappiness is etched in his face. When he is joined by Gabriel's Astrov they are two hopeless men together, bitter but, by showing their small foibles, somehow lovable and occasionally funny.

As the play progresses the whole cast becomes more liberated. Now the adrenalin is flowing, not because of nerves but because the characters of the play take over from the actors; it is now their drama, their sadness or happiness that drives the action.

Auberon and Storm are magnificent together; it is a pleasure to watch the chemistry between the experienced actor and the young newcomer as they feed from each other's energy.

In the interval even gloomy Michael doesn't seem gloomy. His usually pale face is flushed as he goes through the dressing rooms encouraging his players.

"It is going well, the audience is responding, you can feel the tension in the house."

The actors feel that his report is genuine not just pep-talk. The gladiators are ready to go out into the arena for the second half.

The scene between Bella and Gabriel is electric. When he takes her in his arms and kisses her the air is sizzling around them; the kiss seems to last longer than before. Bella is feeling dizzy after it, and the air is charged by the energy between their characters.

Evelyn is in the wings watching. Even she feels the heat, and a wave of nostalgia sweeps over her: my God, they are beautiful. How wonderful to feel so young and vibrant and act out those people. This is the real Yelena and Astrov — or perhaps something a bit more, more than just the characters in the play.

Auberon comes off stage after his most dramatic scene; once in the wings, he switches off completely. No method acting for him. He is one of those actors who leaves the audience in tatters and tears but walks away from the scene unscathed: "If I had suffered the agony of Hamlet every night, I'd have died of a heart attack long ago," he is fond of saying. "The actor's job is to affect the audience not himself."

His final scene with Storm's Sonia is truly heart breaking. The balalaika, softly playing a sad Russian melody offstage, adds to the scene's poignancy. Then, the final curtain.

The actors line up to take their bow with satisfaction; everything went without a hitch. Gabriel kisses Bella's hand in the last curtain call which prompts Auberon to murmur: "Are we at the ballet in

Covent Garden? Where are the bouquets?" But the others just laugh. They are happy that they can do it all again tomorrow.

Bella takes special care getting ready after the show. The crushed velvet dress she brought with her from London is hanging in a wardrobe. Bella knows that its turquoise colour suits her well, it enhances the hue of her eyes. The figure-hugging cut is flattering — she had made many a conquest wearing it. She removes her stage make-up but replaces it with a light base, smoky eye shadow and just a touch of a pinkish lipstick. She has the feeling the lipstick might not stay on until the end of the night. Recalling the scene at the curtain call, Bella thinks tonight will be the night.

She decides she will take the initiative and stop playing coy, waiting for Gabriel to make the first move. She feels sure that she's been too cautious, and perhaps Gabriel has taken it as a forbidding sign. Her spirit is soaring and she feels she can take on anything the world throws at her. She flies through the stage door on her way to the restaurant for the first-night party.

In Maidenford only the Indian restaurants stay open after eleven, so the cast and crew are meeting in the Haweli near the theatre. Michael is sitting at the head of the table and greets them all as they come in. Lots of shiny, smiling faces.

It takes ages to order because everyone wants something else and they want to share as well, so working out who has what is not easy. And that is just the drinks. Eventually, everyone is fed and some drink more than others.

Bella is sitting between Michael and Auberon and her heart is bursting. She hasn't felt so happy for years and certainly never felt like this, she reflects, in a television studio. There is something magical about the theatre and the comradeship that forms between a group of people.

She'd been slightly disappointed to find Storm already sitting next to the unreadable Gabriel; maybe she'd taken too long to get ready. But in any case, they'd kept a seat for her between the director and the leading man just as hierarchy would dictate. There was no way to decline that.

Evelyn is sitting at the end of the table, no doubt keeping in mind that she might want to slip away early. Even she catches the general feeling of happiness around the room and feels grateful to be there. Where else could she mix with all these different people with such a variety of ages and backgrounds, yet so united in their effort? Making something together that gives pleasure to at least some people—I am very lucky, she thinks to herself.

Towards the end of the evening Auberon stands up, clinks a glass and makes a speech. He thanks the director and everybody behind the scenes for their help in realising the production. "We all know that we actors are in front, we are the ones seen but we could not have done it without you all," he says and raises his glass. General cheering and shrieking follow.

My God, it is like an awards speech, thinks Gabriel, —I bet he's done it a few times before. Still, he has to admit, it works like a charm. Gabriel passes on these thoughts to Storm, who keeps giggling. She is exhausted by her travelling to London and back, and the excitement of the opening night. The fact that she is sitting next to Gabriel and that he seems to be taking her into his confidence adds to the thrill. The two are behaving like naughty children.

Nobody notices this in the general jollity, except for one pair of eyes that hardly ever leaves them. Bella's. Her first thought had been that the night would be long and she'd have her chance to move over to Gabriel, and together they'd have their gossip and evaluation of the evening as they'd had during the rehearsal period. Instead, Gabriel, who has obviously had a few drinks, is flirting outrageously with Storm and they are clearly having a wonderful time, meaning Bella is going to have less and less chance to transplant herself from her seat.

The evening is slowly winding down. People start to leave and there are lots of emotional hugs as if they were not meeting again in eight hours' time. Evelyn leaves first; young Amanda gallantly offers to walk home with her and she accepts happily. Now only about half of the seats are occupied around the table and Michael and Auberon are getting ready to leave.

Bella's brain is ticking twice as fast as its normal speed. She has to decide whether to go gracefully with them or walk up to Gabriel and Storm who seem to be totally absorbed in each other's company. She can't just give up yet, so she bids goodnight to her director and Auberon and summarily walks up to Gabriel.

"Just want to say goodnight to both of you, it was fun to relax here after our efforts," she lies. Gabriel looks up and smiles that incorrigible naughty smile of his and asks: "You are going already darling? Well, thanks for everything, thanks for being a great partner." Bella catches her breath—maybe she wasn't altogether wrong—then Gabriel carries on, "We are staying a bit longer, we have to finish this wine you see," and points at a half-empty bottle.

"Yes, good night Bella, sleep tight," grins Storm, with an almost imperceptible wave of her hand.
Bella pulls herself together, kisses Storm and says good night. She is about to hug Gabriel but he has already turned away and is pouring wine. There is no alternative but to make a dignified exit while the

remaining people are shouting good night to her. She realises she ought to have ordered a taxi but now it is too late to turn back. It is not far to go; she will have to walk. The high-heeled shoes are hurting and the bloody velvet dress is too tight. She just wants to fall into her bed. Not quite the evening she'd anticipated.

There is hardly anyone left in the restaurant, but Gabriel and Storm are still sitting at the table. In front of them several empty wine bottles — how many have they finished between them? But Storm doesn't feel tired anymore and it seems to her that the more wine she drinks the clearer her head is. The secret crush she's had on Gabriel has turned into reality. He sits next to her, his arm around her chair; he leans over to face her and he talks and talks incessantly. Storm is not sure what it is he is saying but she nods enthusiastically and occasionally touches his arm to encourage him. Not that he needs encouragement. Gabriel's eyes are burning and he is in an ebullient mood. He doesn't take his eyes off Storm, as if the rest of the room didn't exist, and he is explaining his various theories of acting, though as far as Storm is concerned, he could be quoting from a recipe book.

She is thinking life should stop now! I am on stage in a great part. I know I am good in it. I've just had a film audition and I don't care whether I get it or not, and I have this gorgeous man looking into my eyes and giving his undivided attention to me all evening. There is just a tiny moment of prickly doubt when she remembers Bella, and how Gabriel and Bella were always huddled in a corner in heavy discussion. This is youth's triumph over experience, she thinks cheekily.

She notices that Gabriel has stopped talking; the room is almost empty now, a few waiters are hovering sleepily hoping to close and go home. It is time to make a move but who is going to create the choreography?

Gabriel rises and holds his hand out, "I'll take you home Zozo, to that luxurious abode of yours."

"Should you be driving?" asks Storm, melting inside that he's remembered her pet name.

"I am fine, I'll be fine once I'm in the fresh air. We have to walk back to the theatre where my car is."

Storm just follows him in a trance. They are holding hands as they walk back to the car. Indeed, Gabriel seems very sober now as he walks with determined steps but never letting go of Storm's hand.

The car stops in front of Storm's house. It is dark; the other tenants must have gone to bed early; no student is burning the midnight oil. Gabriel reaches for Storm and starts kissing her. His breath is slightly sour from the alcohol, but Storms finds it masculine and exhilarating. She breaks away and makes a quick decision, "Do you want to come in for a coffee? Might do you good before you drive further," she says in an almost steady voice.

He doesn't even answer just gets out of the car. For a moment he has to let go of her hand, but he grabs it as soon as he can. They climb the stairs and arrive out of breath at the attic room. It is in some disarray, but Storm scoops the clothes up from the bed and throws them down in the corner. They both sit on the bed and just look at each other. Both are smiling, Gabriel even shakes his head a little as if to say: how incredible that we are here, but what have we been doing for the last four weeks?

Coffee is forgotten—who would want to go two floors down to the freezing kitchen? Gabriel slowly starts to undress the girl. The moments are precious and he doesn't want to rush. They are sitting on the bed and locking their gaze deep into each other.

Suddenly there is a strange scratching noise from the corner of the room. They both stop and listen.

"It's nothing, they are my pet mice, well, not mine it is a long story," says Storm, laughing.

"Your what?" Gabriel is aghast.

"They are pet mice, they are sweet, all white, do you want to look at them?"

"No, I don't. Come here, you strange, weird creature, I don't think I have ever made love with mice in a room." He scoops Storm into his arms and they both fall on the bed entangled.

The Day After

Evelyn is just coming round to consciousness after a long disturbing dream. She has these vivid dreams but, oddly, they always involve some theatrical setting. Though maybe not so odd—after all that is her life.

She is invariably young in the dream and at the brink of some disaster. This morning in her dream she was acting in the play St. Joan. She was about to go on stage when she told her colleague, playing Dunois, that she was not sure of her lines but couldn't find her script. But the actor took her by the arm and propelled her towards the stage. A sudden thought came to her that she was too old to play St. Joan—it had been many years since she'd played the part. But an odd-looking stage manager, with a stooping back, materialized and urged her to go on. "At least let me look at your script," she whispered; but when she looked into the prompt corner, instead of the usual copy of the script, there was only a bunch of roses on the prompt desk. "The roses are for me, I am sure," she thinks, "but I'm not going to deserve them. I can't go on, I can't."

She is covered in sweat and her heart palpitating. Then she wakes.

After a few deep breaths she realises where she is and the nightmare was just that, a figment produced by a small part of her brain that is stuck in theatre hell.

She draws the curtains and looks through the window. It is a horrible day outside; it's raining the type of rain that seeps into your bones from under the umbrella. Anyway, that is how Evelyn is feeling, though she hasn't even been outside yet.

There is no point getting up, she thinks, and crawls back to bed. She will miss breakfast but she can treat herself to a little lunch at the Italian Trattoria near the hotel.

It feels good being back in bed and remembering how well the show went last night. She did not disgrace herself, did not make a single mistake, was uplifted by the general excitement and enjoyment of the others. Even the after-party was pleasant.

That stage manager girl, Amanda, was awfully nice, asked her a lot of questions about her past in the theatre and at the end walked home with her. There are some genuinely nice people around, even in the self-focused theatrical profession.

There was one curious thing though. She had been convinced that something was going on between Bella and Gabriel, but last night she couldn't work out what could have happened. Gabriel had been all over Storm during the party and she could see that the girl was beside herself with happiness. She'd seen it all happening before in companies and she could only draw one conclusion: men are scoundrels. Maybe that was too old-fashioned a word but she was reluctant to use the word bastard, though it could be fitting. She wonders now how the evening progressed after she'd left the restaurant. Not that she likes that sort of gossip…but she is intrigued.

Suddenly, she feels very content. How lucky she is that she is in the position still to observe all human foibles. If she wasn't working she would be stuck at home and never be in contact with living, breathing creatures unless they were on television.

She stretches in the bed and gives herself a treat by picking up her book and reading a little more. This is usually an evening occupation but today she spoils herself, and she will have a nice lunch too.

In the Italian restaurant there are only a few people at lunchtime, so there are plenty of tables to choose from. Yet, when she asks for a table for one the waiter offers her the smallest table by the door.

"Could I sit in that booth over there?" she asks, surprising herself.

"But that is for four, as you can see," says the waiter in an accent she can't quite place.

"It is already two o'clock; I don't think you'll have many more customers," she says and walks determinedly to the table. The waiter shrugs and removes the three obsolete covers.

Having ordered a starter and a main dish with a nice glass of red Merlot, Evelyn is in a good mood. She smiles at the waiter who now seems more accommodating towards the elderly lady.

"I love Italy, I've had my best holidays in Tuscany," she says, striking up a conversation. "Which part of Italy are you from?"
"I am not from Italy, I am from Albania."

Evelyn is silent; she'd have been happy to chat about any number of countries but has absolutely nothing to say about Albania.

"Ah, I see a long way…no, I have never been to Albania," she says.
"Not many people have."
The waiter walks away with the dirty plates.

When paying, Evelyn gives him a good tip as compensation for being from Albania.

When she gets back to the guest house a letter is waiting for her. It is her appointment for her brain scan. Even this unpleasant prospect doesn't change her good mood.

What if the machine does not find a brain there? she thinks, and smiles at her own poor joke.

The weather outside is grey and it starts drizzling but Evelyn doesn't mind. Her thoughts turn towards evening when she can get to the theatre, the place where the weather is always the same and the well-lit dressing room with mirrors always provides a haven. When she is away from it, she feels a longing, akin to homesickness — it is the cocoon most actors crave. And she is lucky enough that, for weeks now, she can be in that protective bubble.

Bella gets to the theatre early for the second performance after the opening night. She does not agree with actors who maintain that the second show is often flat because after the excitement of the première it is an anti-climax. She relishes the fact that she can improve on yesterday's performance and correct the small mistakes. She will try to improve until the very last show.

She is obviously disappointed about the happenings at the after-show party, but she can't quite forget that she will be on stage again where Gabriel has to be captivated by her. And not just tonight but for every day of the run. What she saw yesterday between Storm and Gabriel could be down to her imagination, and drink! On their part of course, not hers.

At that moment she hears Gabriel's voice from the corridor. "Is Storm in?"

Oh well. During rehearsals it had always been Bella he'd sought out, even during the dress rehearsals. What had happened, had she done anything wrong? Had she upset him in some way?

From the corridor she can hear the fresh young voice, "I am in here with Evelyn!" Storm shares a dressing room with Evelyn — only Bella and Auberon have their own dressing rooms in this production. At least Gabriel can't do much canoodling in front of the old lady, Bella thinks. She hears the dressing room door close. There is lots of muffled laughter seeping through the walls.

Bella looks contemplatively at her attire. She is in her underwear, a black bodysuit which she thinks is called a 'teddy'; it is just like a swimming suit but it has lots of lace on it. She'd bought it specially, during the dress rehearsals, thinking she would wear it in the dressing room under her silk dressing gown. She'd imagined how her dressing gown would be slightly open to show off the garment when Gabriel came in. She looks in the mirror and the word that comes to mind is enticing — even if that's her own opinion. But it seems now as if the desired audience is not going to attend the performance.

"How stupid" she is muttering to herself.

In the mirror she studies her face. Should she have gone ahead with that plastic surgery? A few months ago she'd visited a plastic surgeon asking for an opinion—should she have some 'work' done? The doctor had told her that all women arch their brows and tighten their facial muscles when they look into the mirror and, therefore, they never have a true image of themselves. She notes with amusement that he was right, as she lifts her head a little to eliminate the suggestion of a slight double chin forming below her jawline. But the worst had been when the surgeon had taken a small wooden stick and sort of rolled her skin up above the eyes. This was another area he could help with, he suggested.

But Bella couldn't commit. She'd seen so many surgeries go wrong—when the person perhaps looked younger but did not look like themselves anymore. Those stretched faces and goggling eyes! Bella decided to grow old gracefully, but not just yet! Oh please, not yet. She takes her face into her hands and stretches the skin—the eyes, the neck are smooth again...then she lets go, with a deep sigh.

Her dresser, an elderly lady, arrives with her blouse that Bella wears in the second act. It is freshly washed and ironed.

"And how are you today, my dear?" but without waiting for an answer the dresser continues: "The buzz is fantastic — the whole town is saying that the theatre has a big success on its hands."

Bella smiles. It is a mystery where this unassuming little lady gets her information, but she has been in this theatre for many, many years and her gossip is hardly ever wrong. Of course, she goes from dressing room to dressing room and picks up all the news, professional and personal. People don't stop talking in front of her; for actors and directors she is just like wallpaper — the aristocracy must treat their servants like this — but she absorbs everything.

The performance goes well tonight. Bella cannot detect any change in Gabriel's ardour in the scenes. He is a fine actor and he is just doing a professional job, thinks Bella with a slight bitterness.

She notices that while Storm stands in the wings, Gabriel passes her and just touches her cheek ever so slightly, as you might touch a pretty child. A small gesture, but Bella sees the significance of it. In this world every look, every small touch, has meaning.

Bella swallows her disappointment, she is still looking forward to the forthcoming shows. She wants to carry on, be alive on that stage.

The Press Night

After four performances it is time for press night. All sorts of rumours are flying about important critics who are coming to see the play. Bella doesn't want to think about them; the less she knows the better. Storm hardly knows anybody's name, only she wants them all to come and see her performance, whoever they are. She feels pretty sure of herself and can't wait to show off to anybody who cares to look.

Storm doesn't understand why her colleagues are so tense. After all, they've already had four performances following the opening night; all they have to do is repeat the same thing again. In fact, this is not correct—she feels that tonight she can be even better because she has to impress. That is why she is here.

Bella feels just the opposite. Suddenly, she has no confidence at all, despite everybody telling her that she has found a new freshness in the character and that she plays Yelena strong and confident, until the overwhelming feeling for Astrov takes hold of her. Aha, and they believe that is great acting, she thinks to herself with sarcasm.

It doesn't help that her husband is watching tonight. Theo has always been her kindest critic, reinforcing her confidence, clever with his suggestions.

Often, although not being in the profession, he notices nuances that the professionals miss. But it has been a long time since he has seen her on stage. Lately, he's become less observant and more absorbed in his own work. She finds that for some reason she is not looking forward to his comments, despite them being given with the best of intentions.

As if all this pressure wasn't enough, her agent is in the audience tonight. Unlike Theo, he seldom has any opinion himself. In his case, the question is will the general atmosphere be good and will he be surrounded by people who are pleased with the production and, crucially, with his client's performance. If so, then the endeavour will be a triumph in his mind.

Gabriel feels Bella's unease and hugs her in the wings. All through the play his energy is glowing so that it feels like he is holding Bella in his arms without touching her. Their very last scene when Astrov declares his love seems to take place on another plane. According to the script, Yelena resists him until the very last moment, when she throws herself into his arms. Bella clings to Gabriel and the embrace lasts a beat longer than before but both feel as if they have added five minutes to the play.

After the last curtain call the company disperses. Enough people have booked tables in the local Italian restaurant to make it worthwhile for them to keep open for a few extra hours.

Bella, her husband, and her agent have reserved a table for three. There are some other cast members' partners and acquaintances in the restaurant who have come for the press night. They all wave to each other, then turn back to their own party.

Bella's husband and agent are of the same opinion that the show is excellent; they both feel that it will have a positive effect on Bella's career. They order champagne and Bella relaxes. She is filled with a warm glow that she is among her own people, on her own turf, in her comfort zone.

They've just clinked glasses filled with bubbly when the door opens and Gabriel comes in with an attractive young woman. She is almost as tall as him and the first things Bella notices about her are her long, crimson nails. Bella takes small, short breaths; she has difficulty continuing the conversation.

Gabriel and the woman sit down at a table, which is right opposite Bella's. This is unfair, she thinks. I was just having a good time, I'd just managed to forget about him and then he walks in, and with an unknown woman. Who can she be? The only positive thing that she can think of is that at least it is not Storm.

Bella needs all her acting talent to keep up a reasonable conversation without taking her eyes off

Gabriel. Meanwhile, he is behaving rather strangely. He does not look at Miss crimson nails; he seems quite detached from her, almost annoyed and instead looks at Bella all the time. As if he had some reason to question her. As if it was Bella who was being provocative, just sitting there, with her own husband and agent.

Gabriel doesn't order any food, just a bottle of wine. At Bella's table the food arrives. When she'd ordered her dish she'd felt ravenous, but now that the food is here in front of her, her stomach feels tight and she has lost her appetite. She is toying with her fork, twisting the pasta left and right but hardly putting any in her mouth. Theo asks: "Aren't you hungry darling? I haven't mentioned it but you have lost a bit of weight, haven't you?"

"Yes," says her agent enthusiastically, "she looks fabulous!"

In his book skinny equals beautiful, much easier to promote slim ladies than plump ones.

Bella ignores the compliment; she knows precisely why she has lost weight.

Meanwhile it seems Gabriel is annoyed with the woman and is keeping his gaze on Bella. There is longing in those eyes, occasionally a slight smile playing on his lips. This is the look that Bella finds so hard to resist. She is yearning to rise, go over to Gabriel's table and challenge him. Why are you looking at me like that? What is the game you are playing? But, of course, she stays sitting and contributes to the discussion on the chances of the show moving into London.

Her agent is convinced that this production with this cast would be a success in town. He promises to make phone calls to the right people about it, and suddenly Bella is animated. Yes, the show must go into town; she is very keen; she wants to do it; she wants a long run.

Her husband is slightly surprised. Until now Bella has always said that long runs would bore her—she preferred the immediacy of filming. Oh no, says Bella, there is nothing like the companionship that forms within a theatre company. And her eyes are shining.

Bella is intrigued. How come the woman does not slap Gabriel for blatantly not looking at her at all, but instead sitting with his eyes fixed in the distance? She is sitting with her back to Bella but she must have noticed that Gabriel is absent from their conversation.

The men at Bella's table are about to tuck into the tiramisu when Gabriel waves to the waiter, pays the bill and rises. The woman seems reluctant to go but Gabriel has a blank expression. Then he walks to Bella's table and says: "Don't want to interrupt, just like to say, Bella, you were magical tonight, wasn't she?" He takes in the men at the table. "I cannot wait

143

to get back on the green. Goodnight all." And that devilish smile is back on his face, his head shaking slightly as he walks out of the restaurant, followed by his mysterious date.

Bella is longing to be in his arms. Now, for the first time, she realises the similarity between her character, Yelena, and herself. They are both married to an older man, a professor, and Bella wishes, as Yelena might, that right here and right now the professor might be swallowed up by the earth. And then she would be free. Dear Theodor, I am sorry…She is ashamed of her own thoughts.

She controls herself and remains seated. What is wrong with Gabriel that he only gives these seductive signs when it's impossible for Bella to respond? And yet it gives her hope. If he can look at her like that, she simply has to wait for the right moment.

The Run Starts

Evelyn has settled into a comfortable routine. She lazes in bed in the morning, has a nice light lunch and spends the afternoon reading or going for a healthy walk, weather permitting. Then in the evening she goes to the theatre. She is always early, usually the first to arrive out of the whole cast. She knows everything she does takes more time than it used to, therefore she treats herself to a leisurely preparation.

When she arrives at the stage door there is a letter for her. The address is handwritten and has no stamp on it. She is puzzled — she doesn't know anybody in this town. Other actors do get fan letters from the local audience but how likely is that in her case?

She is anxious and looks at the letter with trepidation. She is not used to getting good news. With slightly shaky hands she takes the letter and the key to her dressing room and makes her way to her sanctuary.

She unlocks the door; it is dark in there. It will be ages before Storm arrives or, as Evelyn likes to think, 'storms' in. She puts on the lights and sits down in front of her mirror. On her dressing table everything has its place. Every little tube or box has a history and they must travel with Evelyn to every single job. They are part of her wellbeing in the theatre. Some of the tubes are almost dry and some of the potion boxes haven't been opened for years. But you never know what the next role will require, so they remain in Evelyn's collection and they occupy the same position as always.

There are also a few small objects, her mascots. A knitted fox that was given to her by her first boyfriend; it is holding a gosling a bit worse for wear. She used to think that he was the fox and she, Evelyn, the goose. There is also a miniature porcelain chamber pot, with a note inside: *Stay calm. Never wet your pants.* That was from her mother.

After she has surveyed it all and is satisfied that everything is in order, she turns her attention to the letter. Before opening it she looks at the handwriting which is not familiar.

She sees large letters, hurried writing and the page starts without an address.

I don't think you'll remember me, you certainly have not seen me since I was three years old. I am studying here at Maidenford College, and I was so pleased to see your name on the theatre posters. I am your granddaughter!
I am coming to see you tonight in the play and I was hoping that we could meet afterwards. I shall wait at the stage door. I'll understand if you don't want to see me because of family things, in which case please leave a note at the stage door and I will not wait for you.

But I do hope we can meet. I always wanted a granny!
Love,
Susanna, your granddaughter

Evelyn's heart is palpitating as if she has just had one of her disturbing dreams. Can this really be happening? Little Suzy, now Susanna, is reaching out for her and finally she will have some family? Of course, she can't expect a relationship. Maybe, they'll just meet the once and each will go their own way. She is wondering what might she look like? Like her mother? Or maybe she'll have a few traits of her grandmother? Could she look a bit like her? Evelyn's thoughts are running away with her.

She only realises when Storm arrives that she has no make-up on yet and her wig is still pinned on the wig stand. She quickly pulls herself together and starts to get ready. She will really have to give a flawless performance tonight.

Evelyn is in a daze as she is standing in the wings to make her first entrance. As she is moving to the stage, she realises that she hasn't brought her handbag with her. It is not that important, but she has some little business with the bag — she usually gets a hanky out to mop her brow. Well never mind, nobody will notice that she's left it behind.

She is on now and feels that, no matter how full the theatre is, she is giving her performance for one person, one person only.

The show is over very quickly for her. She just about notices that Storm is in a buoyant mood. The young girl chatters with great enthusiasm but Evelyn just nods and says yes or no, hoping that it is the right answer.

She removes her stage makeup but powders her face lightly. She regrets that she is not dressed smarter, but at least she has her trusted navy skirt and jumper on, though, sadly, no jewellery. She's got used to not bringing anything valuable into the dressing room and, as far as costume jewellery goes, she always loses everything.

She is ready to glide through the stage door. As she steps out onto the dark street for a moment, she sees nothing. Then she hears a cheerful voice that doesn't sound entirely unfamiliar — children often inherit the speech patterns of their parents. Then she notices a very tall girl standing alone a few steps away from the stage door. The girl moves towards her.

"Suzy?" whispers Evelyn, and stands a bit uncertain about the next move.
"Evelyn!" says the skinny tall girl who is opening her arms for a hug.
The hug lasts just a bit longer than is comfortable on the street. Evelyn is glad that it is dark because her eyes are welling up.

"Goodness you are tall." She pulls herself together. "Or am I very small? I've probably shrunk."

"Wow, I have a grandma," shouts Suzy "and she is on the stage and she is famous!"

"Famous no, not famous but on stage indeed, just about, hanging on - by a thread" she adds with the help of her professional comedy timing.

"We must go and sit down somewhere," she continues "I would take you out for a meal, but I am afraid my little Italian is now closed."

"Yea, the Maidenford night life! But, if you don't mind, I know a café which is open, really very studenty but there is not much choice." And she takes Evelyn's arm and starts walking briskly.

The old lady keeps up because suddenly she feels ten years younger. She has a bit of a shock when they arrive at the café. It is completely dark outside; you would never go in if you didn't know about the place. Once they step inside the noise is considerable. Groups of young people are sitting at large round tables covered with beer bottles. Suzy waves to a few people and ushers Evelyn into a smaller back room, where it is quieter but almost completely dark, save for a few candles burning.

"I hope this will do, at least we can hear each other speak."

"Oh, this is fine. Very atmospheric." Evelyn is still in shock.

"What would you like? I'm afraid I have to go and get it from the bar — there is no service at the tables."

"Oh, I don't know." Evelyn is out of her depth "What are you going to have?"

"Normally, I have beer, but today I want to celebrate — shall I get us two glasses of wine?"

"That will be great." Evelyn is reaching for her purse but Suzy stops her. "It is absolutely on me, I insist." Evelyn nods. "Red or white?" "Red please."

Evelyn is completely overwhelmed by the assured and grown-up behaviour of her granddaughter. Of course, she is grown up. She must be…what, nineteen or maybe twenty? Suddenly she cannot remember. In her mind she sees only a toddler she can't equate with this willowy girl. She didn't have a chance to look at her face in the dark street, and only fleetingly now. She thinks she's seen traces of her daughter, but Suzy has more regular features, a real English Rose. Ah, Evelyn remembers, that is what they called her when she was young, English Rose.

Suzy is back with the wine and some crisps.

"Sorry, this is all they had. I thought you might be hungry after such a long show."

"Don't worry, I never eat after the theatre, it is not healthy." She doesn't want to sound preachy, so she adds quickly "for such an old lady. Did you find the play long?"

"Not in a bad way, no, I did enjoy it—I should have said straight away. But they do whinge quite a bit, don't they, in the play, I mean?"

"Yes, they do that," says Evelyn laughing.

"But you were very good, though I don't know why you always take the side of that pretentious professor?"

"Well thank you, it is not a role you can do an awful lot with. A bit pretentious herself. You know, when I was younger, I did play much better parts."

"Oh, I know. Although you didn't see mum, she always kept an eye on your work. Sometimes, she would even cut out some reviews to show me."

"Really?" This was bitter-sweet news for Evelyn. So her daughter still thought about her—yet every time she'd tried reconciliation, she'd come up against a hard wall.

"I think she was secretly proud of you," says Suzy.

"Then why...but we should talk about you, what are you studying, why Maidenford, what is happening in your romantic life? I want to know everything."

They talk and talk, and time passes quickly. Evelyn forgets her aches and pains and her forthcoming health checks; she is happy to be in this smoky dark hole with her grandchild, the granddaughter she never thought she would see again.

Storm gets news from her agent that she has a recall for the film role. They want to see her on camera with some male actors, to see what chemistry there might be between them. This time they give Storm enough notice and they book her for a morning session, allowing her to get back for the evening performance. Storm has been so absorbed in the play that she has nearly forgotten about the project. In fact, she wanted to forget about it. Her idea was to banish it from her mind, then there would be no disappointment. But now that she has been called back, it is more difficult not to hope and not to imagine what would it be like if she did get that role; it just might change her life.

This time she calls her mother to say she is going to stay overnight before her audition. "That's fine," says her mother "and how is the play going?"

"It is going fine, mum I did ask you to the opening night but I didn't hear from you," Storm says rather grudgingly.

"Well, you know how it is, always a lot to do, but you can tell me all about it, what the play is and everything."

"Yes mum, see you." Storm hangs up. What does she mean what the play is? She has told her everything about it, explained about the character of Sonia and now mum hasn't got a clue?

It is true that her mother was always against her going to drama school but, by now, she must have realised that her daughter has made a good, if rather lucky, start in the profession. It hurts Storm that her mother does not appreciate and is not interested in what she is doing. Maybe if she could get a role in Coronation Street she would change her mind. Or a Hollywood blockbuster would be handy too.

Storm decides not to tell anybody about the recall, though she cannot stop herself sharing the news with Gabriel. He says he is delighted and crossing fingers and everything else for Storm to get the part. Just for a second a thought as light as a butterfly's wing brushes over Storm: Is he sincere? Is he envious? No, Gabriel seems genuinely pleased.

After the show Storm takes the train to London and arrives at her mother's home just after midnight.

Her mother is up waiting for her. She even has a comforting bowl of soup ready.

"Thank you, mum, that is really nice." With the taste of the soup Storm is back in her childhood, when her mother, now elderly, could comfort her in any situation. Now she seems almost like a stranger. When she offers her cake, Storm says no.

"Sorry mum, I have to get up at 6 tomorrow so I'd better go to bed now."

"You arrive after midnight and you leave at 6? It was hardly worth coming home then!"

"I am sorry—I told you I was not coming home exactly, I just needed a bed for the night."

"What sort of work is it when you have to be available at these unearthly hours?" she says grumbling.

"If I was a nurse working shifts, then would you accept it?"

"That is different, that is something useful."

"Thanks mum, now I am really going to bed. I'm too tired to explain or to argue. Good night."

The following morning, just after six o'clock when Storm emerges from the shower, breakfast is on the table: cereal, a fried egg and toast and steaming coffee. Mum is sitting at the table, and watches Storm eat quickly.

"I thought you'd need something in your tummy. I hope it goes well, whatever you have to do, and do let me know the result."

This time the audition is in the form of a screen test which takes place in a studio. Storm is the only girl in the morning session, which she thinks is a good sign. It is always discouraging to come up against other actresses for the same part, who all seem to be more beautiful, more confident and more suitable for the role. At least today I don't have to sing, thinks Storm — as she fears singing auditions more than anything.

She has to repeat the scene with four different actors. When they see that Storm is staying, while they are replaced, they look at Storm in awe. They assume that she has been cast in the part. After a while Storm herself begins to feel like that. She even affords herself a favourite partner, only silently of course, a young black actor who is obviously hugely talented. I wonder, will he get it? she thinks, forgetting that she's in just as precarious a position herself

At the end of the morning the second assistant informs her that she is finished for the day and can leave. Not a word from the director or the casting director giving any indication of when she might expect some news. But Storm is still on a high and leaves for the train station satisfied. It is only when she is on the train that she starts to wonder — how did she do? She is unable to decide. Had it been any good what she'd done? Had they liked it? Did she have chemistry with any of the other actors? Suddenly she has a strong desire to get the job. She wants it. She imagines filming on foreign locations, discovering 'publicity,' enjoying her agent's sudden appreciation…and she longs for the job! This desire is stronger than anything she has felt before.

As Bella is walking up the stairs to reach her dressing room, she bumps into Gabriel who is racing in the opposite direction.

"Oh you are in early," says Bella, whose throat still tightens when she comes across Gabriel unexpectedly.

"I was looking for you in your dressing room," he says.

"What do I owe the intended visit to?" She tries a little sarcasm, in vain.

"Nothing, just one of our little chats." His eyes are laughing.

"Ok, come in for a little while; you know it takes me ages to make myself look presentable."

"That is a lie, you cannot look anything but presentable."

Bella lets the remark pass unacknowledged.

In the dressing room Gabriel sits down, very relaxed, as if he owned the place. Bella wishes she could find this objectionable but she cannot. In fact, it gives her a comfortable feeling, knowing that he is so relaxed in her company.

She is waiting to hear the purpose of his visit, but Gabriel is not forthcoming. He talks about the play and that in certain parts he feels his performance is slipping, especially when he is on stage with Auberon. Bella suspects that he is suffering from every actor's problem: being on stage with a remarkable actor, knowing fully that the audience cannot take their eyes off that colleague. Bella has no remedy for that but tries to reassure Gabriel that everything is as it should be. He is about to go when Bella can't resist asking: "Who was the lady with you on the press night, at the restaurant?"

"Ahh, just an ex. I find it difficult to get rid of her. I've told her a hundred times that we are over."

Bella doesn't know why but she is pleased to hear this.

"She appeared out of the blue, watched the performance and waited for me at the stage door. I couldn't just walk out on her," says Gabriel with a pained expression.

"Though you obviously did before."

"Well, I did some time ago. But the other night she insisted we have a drink after the show. We were together, on and off, for three years."

"Was that before or after your divorce?"

"After, naturally."

157

"Oh dear, you do have a complicated life."

"Not at all, I just love women."

"No woman wants to hear that Gabriel; you have to make it singular to impress. But go now, I must get ready." Bella makes a reach for her dressing gown.

Damn, she thinks, today I don't have my black lacy underwear on.

So she waits until Gabriel is outside the door, then drops her dress and begins to apply her make-up

Evelyn cannot sleep at night. In the morning she is meeting her granddaughter to give an interview for the University Podcast. It has been ages since anybody has asked her anything. She used to have a definite opinion on all things controversial, but since she has not been challenged for so long, she seems unsure of herself.

Anyway, why would anything she says be interesting for university students? The only thing she has a solid grasp on is the past. But she is still thrilled to be asked. They are meeting in a coffee shop in the centre of town; Suzy will have a colleague with her who will be recording the sound.

Evelyn gets to the meeting place first, settles in a quiet corner and, to her surprise, almost on time, Suzy bustles in. She is followed by a small chap with one side of his head shaved and, on top, a tuft of hair that sits like an electrified brush. He introduces himself as Rob. "Ah," says Evelyn "is that short for Robert or Robin?" "Just Rob," he says and unpacks a laptop and a small microphone. He asks Suzy to pin it on Evelyn's dress.

"My goodness!" Evelyn tries to overcome the awkwardness of the situation "What a tiny mike! In my radio days they used to be enormous."

"We still have all sizes," says Bob the technical wizard, "but this will cut out the surrounding noise."

"Bob is great," says Suzy "he gets us all out of the mess we make on the technical side. He can edit anything and make something out of the most botched material."

"That is reassuring," smiles Evelyn. "What is the laptop for? You are not recording pictures, are you?"

"No, no, but it's easiest to record the sound onto the laptop too."

Evelyn tries to relax. When they are all settled, Suzanna reads an introduction that she has written before.

"We are in the busy centre of town where I am interviewing the veteran actor, Evelyn Blair. She is in Maidenford..."

"Excuse me, don't record what I am saying, but this is one of my hobby horses, I'd like to be called an actress, not an actor. I know that nowadays that is the approved form but I have been an actress for a very long time and I was always proud of my profession and my gender."

"Oh that is great, absolutely great, what a start! Don't stop recording Rob! Just keep it running," Suzy enthuses. "So you don't approve, regardless of gender, of people who are in the acting profession being called actors?"

"I don't disapprove, but I personally have always been proud to be a woman and I think my sexuality was important for me. But if others prefer to be called actors, that's fine. Also, I find it confusing, with names like Glenn and Storm how you are supposed to know what gender they are writing about?"

"Does it matter?"

"I should think it does, yes. Even if the parts are..." Evelyn is searching for the word "...are gender-fluid, now I am yet to see a great female Hamlet. Mind you, even I am not old enough to have seen Sarah Bernhardt."

"Who is Sarah Bernardt, Evelyn? Tell us."

"She was a great French actress in the 19th century. She played Hamlet with a wooden leg."

"Really? That is amazing! And she had a wooden leg?"

"Yes, unfortunately she had to have her leg amputated, but she went back to acting afterwards. Thinking of it just now, she was a disabled actress, that is positive, isn't it? We are trying to be more inclusive in the profession and employ actors with disability." Evelyn is pleased with herself; the conversation is going well.

"Have you thought about what you would have done if you had not become an actress? What other profession?" asks Suzie.

"Oh, I don't know, I was quite an aimless young girl, but a teacher pointed me towards drama school. All very traditional really. I probably would have looked after animals in some way."

"Do you have any pets?"

"No, I'm afraid in this profession—here one day, somewhere else the next—it would not be possible."

Is there anything else on your mind that you would like to share with us?"

"Yes, I do have another hobbyhorse. Why do they call us actors luvvies? Who on earth came up with that expression that no actor ever used? Yes, the word, darling, maybe, especially my generation, but luvvie! Arghh!

Then the talk moves towards the present production: Chekhov and the cast of the play.

"It is so important that you like your colleagues; for me it is a privilege to be on stage with someone like Auberon Hayman. When you are surrounded by talent you have to raise your game." Evelyn is getting into her stride.

"Also, though I would never call myself a feminist, well, why not? I shall call myself a feminist because we have a special bond in this cast. I know that my young colleague can turn to me with anything on her mind – and have done so, and I would go to our leading lady with any of my problems."

They chat on for about a half an hour when Suzy winds down the interview, thanking Evelyn for her time.

When it is all finished, Evelyn is anxious, she is worried she wasn't able to talk of anything interesting. Suzie reassures her that she is delighted and it is important for her and the other kids to hear another's point of view. Evelyn is wondering. She doesn't think she expressed any point of view.

When appearing in a play away from home, once rehearsals are over, you are free all day. You have time to kill until it is time to go to the theatre for the evening show.

To fill their day Gabriel and Storm decide to visit a nearby stately home. They walk in the manicured formal garden hand in hand, and both are surprised at how they got to this state so rapidly. Storm's unconditional adoration and youthful enthusiasm have flattered Gabriel.

It is almost winter now and the garden is not at its best. There are no colourful flowers, and the beds are dormant waiting for next spring. The enormous trees stand with majesty, some leaves still left on their branches in a variation of autumn colours. In a painting it is kitsch, but in nature it is stunning.

As they cross a charming bridge over a fast-flowing brook, they arrive at the wild part of the estate. Here the grass is left to grow and the leaves are not raked or removed. Luckily, there has been little rain lately and the ground is not muddy.

On a small hill there stands a ruin of a chapel. They walk up to it, then stop for a moment, just gazing at each other, as if they had just met, each exploring the face of the other. Gabriel lifts his hand and moves the rogue hair from Storm's eyes. Then gently lays her down on the bed of leaves and kisses her. She kisses him back eagerly.

There are leaves in her hair and she starts giggling. The ground is uneven, and the roots of a tree dig into her back.

"Jesus, who wrote this scene? This supposed to be a romantic interlude, why are you laughing?" Gabriel asks.

"If it is a romantic scene ask the man responsible for props to get us some blankets," says Storm.

"For a brilliant actress, you do have some lousy timing." Now Gabriel is laughing as well.

He helps her up, hugs her and, arm in arm, they decide to explore inside the house. They've bought the tickets, so they might as well.

The mansion is crammed with antique furniture and paintings of varying quality, mainly portraits of the ancestors of the family. They walk through the rooms. If they are honest, they have to admit that neither of them is in the habit of visiting stately homes or even museums often. This was just a way of doing something together. Both are elated that they've decided to come.

In one of the salons, the so-called yellow room, Storm notices a small painting in a corner. A young woman is standing in a yellow dress of the precise style that their play *Uncle Vanya* is set in. Storm blurts out without thinking, "Look, it is exactly like Bella's dress, even the hair is the same!"

There is a moment's silence. Storm is looking at Gabriel for his reaction. She'd never dared to question him about what did happen between him and Bella, if anything.

"That is a lovely painting," he says, "but Bella is more beautiful."
Silence. Storm's female instinct tells her not to continue with the subject.

After they've walked through the house, Gabriel wants to find a nice village pub.
They are just driving around hoping to come across one.

"Shouldn't we have sent somebody on a recce for the next romantic scene?" jokes Gabriel. "It is not the stars' job to find the location."
"Ah, but there is only one star in this car," says Storm.
"Please don't be so conceited!" smiles Gabriel.
"You know very well that I meant you."
"OK, we are not going to fall out over that."
"We are not going to fall out, period." Then a little later in small voice: "I hope."
After a few turnabouts they see a pub sign — Dirty Dick's. "This will do", says Gabriel "it looks perfect."

"How could we go into a place called Dirty Dick's?" asks Storm laughing.

"I hope you don't find any personal connections in the name." Gabriel is mock offended.

When they go in a large lady with a large smile, says "Sorry, kitchen is closed, but I can give you a drink if you are quick."

"A lager and a tomato juice," says Gabriel. "Typical English welcome, no bloody food!"

But even going without food, does not dampen their spirits.

Run interrupted

Evelyn is getting used to the lazy mornings. Why should she hurry to leave her comfy bed when the weather outside is getting colder every day? But this morning she has to get up early; she has a hospital appointment for her scan. She finds any change to her routine more and more difficult to cope with. She slept badly and finds it hard to pull herself together.

She skips breakfast, wraps up well and makes her way to the bus stop. She is surprised to see so many people waiting for the bus. Of course, it is rush hour now; during the day there is hardly anyone waiting at this stop.

She squeezes onto the bus, turning her head to look in case some kind soul might offer her a seat. No such luck. The young ones are all gazing at their phones intently as if there's no life beyond those screens. At the next stop she is pushed further in. A woman with a kind face, who Evelyn judges must be in her fifties, offers her seat. Evelyn hesitates for a moment; this woman should not have to give up her place when all the young men are sitting, but it seems churlish not to accept. Evelyn radiates her most charming smile and murmurs a thank you before sitting down.

The hospital is not far. When she enters, she feels her heart pounding in her chest — so loud, she thinks that everybody must be able to hear it. At reception they direct her to the right area. A nurse comes and fetches her almost immediately; this is going well, she thinks, there was no reason to worry so.

She has to undress and get into a hospital gown. It occurs to her that soon she will be able to play only those roles in hospital beds — the poor woman dying in the corner — in some television series. I wouldn't mind, anything for work, she thinks. After this, I will be able to portray somebody who is pushed into a scanner. How useful will that be!

The radiologist asks her whether she is claustrophobic, as she will have to be very still inside the scanner.

"Would you like some classical music to listen to?" asks the nurse.

"How did you guess I wouldn't want heavy metal?" laughs Evelyn trying to be funny. Neither the nurse nor the radiologist smiles. That went well, thinks Evelyn, no sense of humour whatsoever. They push her into the long tube.

In the first moments Evelyn does feel a touch of claustrophobia but it passes. She is a disciplined person: if she has to be still, she will be still. She closes her eyes and listens to the music. It is Mozart. Finally, something I like. Shame I have to get inside a scanner to hear it, she thinks.

She is so relieved on her way home – the possibility that something might be wrong with her brain never occurs to her. She was told they would let her know the result after a consultant has interpreted the MRI scan.

She is looking forward to ringing her granddaughter; she wants to find out how the podcast went down. She will tell her about her hospital outing. But at the theatre she is not going to tell anybody.

A couple of weeks later, a notice goes up at the stage door for the whole company to be on stage half an hour before the performance. There are different rumours going around about what the meeting is going to be about.

At seven o'clock all cast members and crew are gathering on stage when Michael arrives. He is smiling for once – it looks like he has good news. Auberon is standing next to Bella; he seems to be in a good mood; he is probably familiar with the content of the news already.

Michael speaks; it is with slightly more attack that the company is used to.

"I have good news or, at least, I hope you will be as delighted as I am. After the usual argy-bargy over finding a suitable theatre, it is now confirmed that the production is going to the West End. After we finish the run here, we will have a hiatus, and in March we'll gather together again, and after a week's rehearsal we will open. Obviously, we have had no time to liaise with all your individual agents yet but I sincerely hope that all of you will be free to take part. I consider every member of this company essential and a contributing factor to the success of the production."

General approval comes from every corner of the stage. Bella hugs Auberon with enthusiasm. Evelyn plants affectionate kiss on Storm's icy cheeks. Even though Storm has only returned half of the hundred pounds Evelyn lent her, she has developed quite warm motherly feelings towards her young dressing room companion.

The gaze of Bella and Storm both search for Gabriel's reaction but, to their surprise, he hugs the dear old soul who plays the nurse and leaves the stage.

"Now, please get off the stage as fast as you can, so we can open the house for tonight's audience." With this, Michael wraps up the short meeting.

The run is going well. It's thrilling for the cast to know that they have a success on their hands. The play is regularly sold out and more and more people are coming up from London to see what is happening in Maidenford.

With the show running so smoothly, the actors are not expecting any kind of blip, but during one of the mid-week matinées, in the second act, when Gabriel and Bella are on stage for the night scene, they are caught completely off guard. It is the scene where Gabriel, as Astrov, unrolls a large map, a chart showing how the countryside has changed during the last hundred years. The forest is disappearing and, with it, the wildlife. When Astrov says this is how it was only twenty-five years ago, he points to a part of the map. Today, however, in the matinée, instead of the picture of large trees, there is a drawing with two babies sitting on a potty, holding hands. Their faces are replaced with photos of Gabriel and Bella.

Gabriel and Bella are stunned into silence. They don't dare to look at each other. Instinctively they know the scene is in danger of complete collapse. Gabriel is the one who has to speak first, and it is a long speech. His beard is quivering as he mouths the first words, but, to his credit, he manages to carry on.

Bella is in trouble. A terrible giggler at the best of times, she is almost gone. She turns upstage puts her hand over her mouth and nods from time to time, in a desperate attempt to signal that she is fully engrossed in what Astrov is saying.

Eventually, the scene ends and first Gabriel and then Bella can escape off stage. They are furious but are wiping away tears from holding back their laughter. Not at the joke but from the shock. Who would dare to do such a thing and how did the person get hold of the prop, the map?

It must have been Auberon. No one else would have the audacity or the energy to carry out a prank like that. This is confirmed when they go to their respective dressing rooms — there is a bunch of flowers in Bella's and a bottle of wine in Gabriel's, and a card of apology alongside each. Not placated, Gabriel rushes to Auberon's dressing room to tell him how unprofessional this was and how he nearly ruined the scene completely. But Auberon is like a naughty child: "I only did it because I knew you two would be able to cope with it." Now, though, he relents and says sorry — umpteen times, and the two of them end up laughing.

Bella decides not to give Auberon the satisfaction of enjoying his bad joke, but inside she is just a teeny-weeny bit pleased that he pictured her and Gabriel holding hands.

The day starts badly for Storm. She finally gets the news about her audition for the film role—they'd taken their time telling her agent that they'd decided to go 'in a different direction'. Really! Storm does not think of herself as a direction; she is not left or right, nor up or down. She is a person. What they meant of course was that someone else had got the part. They'd taken their time because until they negotiated the contract with their first choice, they'd left every other possible actor dangling. Every decision serves the production and nothing serves the actor. Storm is a beginner, but she has learnt that much already.

She cannot say much on the phone to her agent—anyway what is there to say? The worrying thing is that every time you are turned down for a part, your agent believes in you a little less.

Storm ends the call, then has a little cry. Afterwards, she reminds herself how she'd felt after the first audition when she hadn't even wanted to be involved. But now, having been through the second audition and with more time to think, she finds she really wants to be in a big Hollywood film.

Her second thought is that she must share this news with somebody. She doesn't want to make a three-act drama out of her disappointment, but she is in need of a sympathetic ear. The obvious choice is Gabriel. But lately something is not quite right with him. For the last two days when Storm has wanted to speak to him, he hasn't answered his mobile.

Storm has let this go since he has been his charming tactile self during the evening performances. No explanation of why he's been so busy or where he has been, but Storm decided not to confront him.

Now with her major news, she wants to talk to Gabriel. His number is on the speed dial but, once more, he does not pick up. Storm has a bitter taste in her mouth. What on earth is he doing during the day? Or maybe he simply wants to let me know that we are over, she muses. She goes for a run then tries his number a few more times without luck. She waits for the evening and, before the show, visits Gabriel's dressing room and tries to drop in casually that she needs to speak to him after the performance. Gabriel looks a bit sheepish.

Good, Storm thinks; he must be thinking that I am going to confront him about my unreturned calls. But I have real news tonight. I will make it sound like I just needed to share it with a more experienced colleague.

After the show, Storm suggests that they go to her place. Even if her room is the shabbiest of all the digs, at least she doesn't have a landlady or a receptionist who watches the comings and goings. Gabriel agrees.

Storm races ahead on the stairs, Gabriel follows at a steady pace. How different it had been the first night they'd come back here together — they hadn't let go of each other's hand even on the narrow staircase. The room is tidy. Storm has expected this visit every single night. There is a bottle of red wine with two glasses on the small table.

Storm opens the bottle and pours without asking him anything.

"Well," she starts with a deep sigh "I didn't want anybody to know in the company, that I've heard that I didn't get the part in the film."

Gabriel looks quite relieved, like somebody who has just received some good news. Evidently, he was prepared for a different conversation. He quickly alters his expression and tries to show some empathy.

"Oh that sucks, but you are so young, it was only your first film audition, you must not take it to heart."

This is the last thing Storm wants to hear. The most infuriating thing is to be told she is young and has time. This is a job for now, and she wants to play it now, while she is young and wants to make a name for herself. And she is disappointed and is hurting, now! She needs someone who can understand that.

Indeed, Gabriel is not stupid, he knows exactly how Storm feels but he cannot find the right words. And somewhere very deep down he feels something that he can't even admit to himself, a tiny scrap of joy that he is not the only one who so far has not been able to penetrate the world of movies. Why is it that a colleague's failure always makes you feel a bit better about yourself?

Storm is disappointed in his reaction and decides to change the subject.

"That is not the only reason why I am upset," starts Storm. "Where have you been in the last couple of days? And why would you not pick up your phone?"

"You have been calling me?"
"Don't pretend that you don't know."
"When?"
"Oh Gabriel, give me some credit, you can make-up any story you like, but not that suddenly your phone wasn't working."
"Did you leave a message?"
"I didn't leave a message every time—the technology of today shows you perfectly well who called you."
"The technology can go wrong."
"Oh please!"

176

"A relationship doesn't mean that I have to account for every minute of my life. Allow me to breathe...I can't abide clinginess."

"I am not asking you to spend all the time with me, but at least you could have spared three minutes for a talk."

Gabriel decides to take the conversation back to Storm's film role.

"You mean you've had this news from the film company for a couple of days? Why didn't you say anything in the theatre?"

"No, I only heard about the film today."

"Then what ...?"

"What? Do I have to have some major news to tell you? I thought..."

At this point Storm is losing her composure. Her instinct tells her that there is no point carrying on with this, she will only lose. Despite her resolve to remain strong, she feels her throat tightening and her eyes smarting; she is close to tears.

Gabriel stands up and takes her into his arms.

"Come on, this is not like you at all. Believe me I know what it is like to lose out on a role. I understand you."

Storm could have screamed. No! I am not crying about the job, I am crying because of your behaviour, because you are betraying me. Maybe not with another person, but you are betraying our relationship and now you want to pretend that I am upset about the film. But she doesn't say any of this. She stays in his arms and buries her sobbing face in his chest.

Gabriel takes her gently to the bed and lays her down. Storm's last thought is: I am a pushover, I have no guts. But she returns his kisses and is grateful that he stays the night.

It is a grey morning. Storm looks out of the window and it is snowing. How unusual to have snow fall this early. Suddenly, the grimy street is transformed. The snowflakes are settling on the bare trees and the branches seem grateful that they have been dressed in glittering white. There is not much traffic in this street—few people have cars. The students are commuting on bicycles and the landladies mostly walk.

Storm glances back to the bed where Gabriel is just turning onto his other side.

"Hey look, it is amazing, there is snow every-where." Storm tries to sound casual, not wanting to give away that last night she had a chilling feeling that their relationship was broken.

As Storm is looking out at the softly falling snow, she is sorry now that she questioned Gabriel. Last night the atmosphere was close to breaking point, until Storm retreated, not being able to bear the thought of losing him. Every atom of her body is trying to resist a relationship where she is the weak one, yet she cannot help it—the attraction is too strong. And perhaps it's okay to appear needy; after all, that is the exact truth, she needs him and wants him.

Unfortunately, this is just the point at which Gabriel usually starts withdrawing from any relationship. He is attracted to the unattainable and Storm has made herself too vulnerable. However, the snow seems to make Gabriel happy too.

He crawls out of bed, pulls his jeans on and they run out into the small garden. Even that neglected corner of the world looks beguiling now. They behave like children, they make snowballs and they chuck them at each other with abandon. Storm gives as good as she gets. They laugh and scream until they are both flushed and thoroughly wet. Time for a hot coffee.

They retreat to her room, where a kettle and some cups make it possible to avoid the communal kitchen. It is pretty basic though. Only the white mice give it some exotic air. They are also reacting to the strange light and the large fluffy crystals coming from the sky, whirling around in crazy circles.

While cuddling their warm mugs they have the same intimacy that they had at the start of their romance. Gabriel sighs and ruffles Storm's sticking-up hair as if he was saying: I still like you, silly kid.

"Shall we go for lunch to the Italian place?" asks Storm but regrets it in the same moment. Again, she is the one who is taking the initiative. "Only if you have nothing better to do," she hurriedly adds.

But Gabriel is in a good mood and agrees. "But before we go to the restaurant we'll have a long walk. Let's go to the park, it must be beautiful there."

Storm is delighted. Who cares about the wretched film if she's got Gabriel?

For a few days, the life of the theatre progresses without any unusual events. One night, at the curtain call Gabriel asks Bella for an after-show drink. Bella is surprised and, more to the point, intrigued.

"Why not? Just a quick one then," she says lightly. "I'll wait for you at the stage door," says Gabriel.

Bella takes a little bit longer than other nights to change, regrets not wearing her flattering high boots instead of the flat, mumsy ones, then makes her way to the stage door. Storm always gets out of the dressing room in minutes, almost bumping into the audience leaving the theatre, so Gabriel waits a few minutes to avoid meeting her. By the time Bella's steps can be heard on the stairs he is standing there, pretending to read the notices on the board.

The pub is quiet; only the serious drinkers are still sitting on bar stools and Gabriel finds a quiet corner table. Bella asks for half a pint.

"I wasn't registering you as a beer drinker," says Gabriel.

"I know, but after the show when one is thirsty that is the best."

"As you wish, my angel," and Gabriel goes up to the bar.

Bella is looking around. A few people in the inner room have obviously been to the theatre — they have programmes in their hand. Some smile at her, knowingly, but are too shy to accost her. Thank God, she thinks. It is all very well having fans, but in some situations it is better to have them at a distance. Is this such a situation? There is nothing wrong with having a drink with a colleague after a performance, so why is she feeling that it's a clandestine rendezvous?

Gabriel returns with the drinks; they both peel off their winter layers and Bella looks at Gabriel directly with open expectant eyes. She is too proud to show how hurt she was by Gabriel ignoring her and flirting or, if rumour has it right, having an affair with Storm. He must not know how she feels about him.

"Great about the transfer," starts Gabriel on a neutral subject. "It is important because the only work that gets noticed is in London," he adds somewhat bitterly.

"That is unfortunately true," admits Bella. She waits patiently for Gabriel to bring up the subject of why they are here. She is not going to make it easier for him.

Gabriel takes a long slow sip of his beer. "I wanted your advice on something."

Aha, thinks Bella, it will be something to do with London—publicity, accommodation or agents. But Gabriel comes out, unexpectedly, with: "I have a problem with Storm."

"Oh, I am sorry to hear that," says Bella, with just a little thrill of pleasure.

"I am not sure how to handle the situation," Gabriel continues. "I don't want to hurt her. At the same time, the longer we go on, the more difficult it will be."

"What makes you think that I would have an answer?"

"I'm not sure, but you and I have had such great talks, I've always felt we were on the same page."

Bella is pleased to hear that, while at the same time knowing that they were absolutely not on the same page, as Gabriel put it. Her voice becomes one of empathy, not that Gabriel would notice.

"What seems to be the trouble? I thought you were getting on very well."

"Yes, we were to start with. I was just heady and excited at first—her youth was obviously appealing, but it just didn't...I think we were carried away with the play, the success of it, that we were part of something thrilling..." Gabriel is not sure how to go on.

Bella has to pull herself together to maintain her councillor tone.

"So, what has changed?"

"I don't know. All I know is that she wants more commitment; she wants to spend all our spare time together, and I am not able to do that."

Bella is quiet. Gabriel goes on after a pause: "It is not the first time this has happened to me. I am not the type to commit. I feel trapped."

"Well, you should never feel trapped in a relationship that isn't right."

Bella knows that she is flattering Gabriel. This is not what she should be saying. What she should be saying is: something is clearly wrong with you; you play with women and when you have had enough you get rid of them. And Storm is just your next victim.

But Gabriel grows in confidence from Bella's words.

"She is suffocating me; she calls several times a day; if I don't answer, she goes into a meltdown."

"That is not good for either of you.. You must find a way to calm her down. Look, she is very young..."

"I know she is young, but she is no wilting flower, you know—she has a forceful nature."

"I think it is just bravado; underneath she is a naïve young girl."

"She knows well what she wants."

"And that is you," says Bella with a smile.

Gabriel shrugs then grins, as if he is saying it is not my fault that I am so irresistible.

"Listen Gabriel, be gentle with her; tell her that it is over. It is better that way than both torturing yourselves. As we said, she is young, which means it will be easier for her to move on."

Bella is not proud of herself at this moment; she is letting down the 'sisterhood'.

Gabriel reaches for her hand, squeezes it and gives her one of his chocolaty looks.

"It is so easy with you. I am lucky to be your friend."

The word punches Bella in the stomach. Yes, friend; I am a friend and a mate, but I pay a price for that. For you to look at me like that, I have to accept being a friend. So as not to make a fool of myself, I must go along with being your friend.

"Are you looking forward to the run of the play in town?" asks Bella because at this moment all she can think about is the forthcoming performances and the joy of being on stage with Gabriel every night.

"Do you think we will be as successful in the West End as we are here? I've noticed that when shows transfer, they often find themselves judged harshly by the London critics," says Gabriel.

"Oh, we shouldn't think about the critics; we'll enjoy playing for ourselves and the audience who turn up on the night."

"You are right of course."

They finish their beer and Gabriel drives Bella to her hotel.

"I am not coming in tonight, but thanks ever so much for being so understanding."

"Of course," says Bella, thinking who asked you to come in tonight? No need to make an excuse. She plants a kiss on his cheeks and gets out of the car. She goes inside with dance-y steps in her mumsy boots.

Before the Tsunami

Bella is enjoying the run. Some actors get bored by repeating the same show night after night. She is not one of them. There is a different audience every night and the performance becomes different accordingly. They are not big changes just nuances but they keep the play fresh. Occasionally, a line or a situation seems new to the player and, suddenly, it becomes clear that this is the only way to play it. Bella loves those moments.

The dressing room becomes more of a second home. Bits and pieces gather, and an extra piece of make up or a cushion for the uncomfortable chair makes it like nest building.

Bella hasn't felt so free with her time since she was a young student. In London she is always busy. Various commitments springing from her television fame fill the day. And there is Theo. She enjoys making him his favourite dish for dinner or listening to him reading his lectures. She doesn't understand all of it, but his warm voice gives her a feeling of comfort. She can also be helpful in clearing up obscure passages with her logical questions.

Now there is none of these things. No cooking, no reading together, no watching television with Theo. It is all different.

In the hotel every morning there is a keep-fit class that the employees organised for themselves. Before the dining room opens for breakfast, they push the tables and chairs together and a teacher comes in to give a class. Bella joins these classes at least three times a week. The waitresses and the reception crew — naturally they are all women attending these classes. Bella is wondering, are men simply lazy? — are thrilled that they have a celebrity among them. They sent her a stunning bouquet of flowers for the opening night, which gave Bella more pleasure than all the other flowers. Well, almost all.

In the theatre, everyone knows that Gabriel and Storm are in a relationship. Not that anyone cares much; it is just one of those things that happens in companies. Of course, Bella cares. Obviously, the others have no knowledge of Gabriel's intention of breaking up with Storm — if he is going to break up with her, that is. Bella knows that he is capable of keeping more than one woman yearning for him. Like those jugglers with plates in the circus...but then some of the plates fall down and break occasionally. She is hoping that this will not happen to Storm. It would be a great pity for her to be damaged so early in her promising career.

Bella almost forgets how the relationship between Gabriel and Storm hurt her. Deep in her heart she feels she is the one who should have been having that affair.

Or maybe it would be over by now? But might there be another chance, a possibility? Maybe she did something wrong? Should she have been more forthcoming? On the screen she often plays the *femme fatale*, yet in real life she could not do it. Or is she simply too old now?

She still loves her scenes with Gabriel. On stage nothing has changed: the dark eyes are still burning, the kisses are real, and Bella thinks herself lucky to be in his arms, even for fleeting moments.

She spends her time reading a lot, browsing in antique shops, and going to the farmer's market to buy fresh fruit. The long walks she used to go for are not so pleasant now. Winter is here and the days are short and drizzly.

After her keep-fit class, she has the luxury of reading the paper every day, an activity she never found time for at home, to Theo's annoyance. This morning it is so cold in the hotel dining room that after class she rushes back to her room, takes a warm bath and in her tracksuit begins to read the paper.

Somewhere around page ten her eyes stop suddenly on a headline. *Famous actor accused of sexual misconduct.* Who is it this time? she thinks, adjusting her reading glasses. *Auberon Hayman, the award-winning star of many acclaimed stage productions is accused of inappropriate behaviour by a woman, who prefers to remain anonymous. The event occurred twenty years ago, when Mr. Hayman was appearing in a play on stage.*

Jesus, not Auberon, it cannot be Auberon. And who is this woman, who hasn't got the guts to reveal her name? These days anybody can accuse anybody — these are the first thoughts in Bella's mind.

Then she lowers her paper and the worm of doubt sets in...What if it is true? Auberon's charm can be cloying sometimes. Maybe too sweet. How is one to know what he was capable of all those years ago?

Bella is feeling sick; it takes only a few seconds to think through all the possible events that might follow. And she cares for Auberon as a colleague and as a friend. She admires him. Her instinct is to protect him, to say that the accusations are false. They must be.

Her memory takes her back to the first time they worked together. She is on stage with him, in a play. Bella was a youngster, Auberon was an established leading man. Did he ever approach her? Does she remember him making any overtures? No, never. Maybe she just wasn't his type. Didn't he fancy her?

Now she feels quite hurt. No, no he was not like that. I would have heard rumours. What is going to happen now?

If her respectable paper is reporting this news what must be written in the tabloids? Should she call

Auberon to give him a chance to explain? She decides it is not her place to interfere. After all, she knows nothing. Should she ring some of her colleagues to warn them? Talk to Gabriel? No, that would be wrong. Maybe the rumour will stop with this small article. She is hoping so with all her heart.

It is five o'clock and so dark it could be the middle of the night. Storm's room is cold but where else can she go? It is too early for the theatre, and she has no friends in this town to have a social life with. Gone is the happy comradeship of the drama school, when there was always somebody to speak to, always a lot to do. Storm is fidgety, finds it difficult to keep still. She decides there is time enough to go for a quick run before the evening performance. She pulls her running gear on and leaves the house.

One side of her brain says it is foolish to go for a run so close to the evening performance. But Storm knows that running is the only activity that calms her down. She wants to give a break to her thoughts. Just concentrate on putting one leg in front of the other, keep a steady pace and her heartbeat will follow the beat of the run and not the erratic painful thoughts in her head.

She has done this run lots of times. There is a small wood near her street; she often runs through it, it takes only a few minutes. She is breathing heavily and runs into the woods. It is not raining but everything is damp, moisture is dripping from the trees. The paths are poorly lit; there is an eery yellow light falling on the narrow asphalt.

Storm thinks she will cut through and will make the woodland part of her run shorter. She turns onto a path on her side which she is sure leads back to a main road. She keeps running and, miraculously, her full concentration is on the run; she is feeling better already.

The short cut she took turns out to be longer than her usual route. The main road fails to materialise, and Storm is getting inpatient. Should she turn back or keep running? She decides to turn back and retrace the route to her street. On the way back she does not seem to recognise her path. There are several turnings off the road she is running on. She looks at her Fitbit watch — she has been running for half an hour and she has no idea where she is. It is getting late. She must get to the theatre in time.

It starts raining, but Storm hardly notices it — she is running faster now. She wants to get out of these wretched woods.

At the theatre the stage manager calls the quarter; everybody should have been at the theatre 15 minutes ago at the latest. Evelyn knows that Storm is the 'last minute girl' but she has never missed the half hour call before. Evelyn has a bad feeling about this and goes in search of the stage manager to report that Storm has not arrived yet. She finds Michael on the stage giving a few technical notes to the stage manager.

Evelyn can see that at first neither of them seems concerned—after all this is Storm who is being late. Evelyn goes back to her dressing room but when, in the next ten minutes, there is still no sign of Storm, her anxiety grows.

Michael is waiting by the stage door; the performance should start in 10 minutes. There is a full house and the options are very limited in terms of what to do if Storm does not arrive. Do they cancel the performance? There are no understudies. Perhaps Amanda, the assistant stage manager could read Sonia's lines. Both choices are dire.

Also, what could have happened to her? She must have had an accident—should they call the police? Michael keeps trying her mobile, but it always goes to voicemail.

Storm is soaked through the skin. She has realised by now that she hasn't got her phone with her. She left the house in a mood and planned to be away no longer than half an hour. She can't phone the theatre, she can't alert anybody. She is beginning to panic.

This is a nightmare. How is it possible? — this whole town can be run through in half an hour. Where the hell am I?

Her run is slowing down. She is getting tired — she feels she is going round in circles. I must get out of these woods, just come to civilisation somewhere; then maybe a taxi...but of course, she hasn't got any money. And even if she had, taxis in Maidenford? People order them weeks ahead if they need to go somewhere.

The clock is ticking, and Storm is getting frantic. She is about to collapse and cry, when she notices some bright lights in the distance. She pulls her last bit of strength together and aims for those lights.

She emerges onto a busy major road. Cars are speeding past, their windscreen wipers racing. She has no idea where she is. She must stop a car but it would be so dangerous. She has to find a junction or a corner where the cars might slow down.

Storm has to make a quick decision which way to run and she chooses left. She gets to a junction and there are some traffic lights. She approaches the waiting cars and starts knocking on their windows. The lights change and the drivers ignore her, speeding ahead. Maybe when the lights next go to red.

At the theatre Michael makes the decision to ask Amanda to read the lines. She will be at the side of the stage with the text in her hand. Michael goes round the dressing rooms and tells everybody what he has decided. The cast can't believe it; they must act opposite a ghostly voice. They are all shattered — wouldn't it be better to cancel the show? Auberon is about to tell Michael he does not want to go on under these circumstances.

At the crossroads, at last, an elderly gentleman winds down his window. Storm explains everything but it takes some time for the man to understand what she wants. "First please, please phone the theatre!" she croaks. The man kindly pulls to the side and lets Storm into his car, though he puts a blanket first from the back onto the passenger seat — he doesn't want the girl to drip on his smart upholstery.

They search on his phone for the number of the theatre and he dials. They can only get to the box office but they will pass the message backstage.

"How far are we from the theatre?" asks Storm. "It is only about ten minutes, but could be more in this traffic," comes the answer.
"Tell them to hold the curtain!" Storm shouts. "A kind gentleman is going to drive me there."

The kind gentleman is chuffed to be part of such an exciting off-stage drama. In about a quarter of an hour the car pulls up at the theatre. Michael is on the street waiting for them. Storm darts out of the car, hardly thanking her rescuer; her director has the task of showing gratitude for his kindness. He offers him two free tickets for a performance, which he accepts with pleasure.

A whole team is working on Storm to get her ready for the stage. Dresser, Amanda, Evelyn are all frantically towelling her dry, pulling her clothes on, brushing her hair. Curtain goes up fifteen minutes late — the show is on!

By the following night the company have recovered from their shock. There is a discreet knock on Bella's dressing room door. Evelyn sticks her head in, "Am I disturbing you?" "Not at all, lovely to see you," says Bella.

Evelyn inches her way in and, for a moment, remembers when she was the one who had the spacious number one dressing room. Bella's scent fills the space; it must be some wonderful French perfume.

There is a couch in the corner of the dressing room. If the number one artist wishes to stretch out or have a nap, this comfort is provided. The rest can sit upright all the time.

Bella points to the couch. "Have a seat." Evelyn perches at the edge of the couch, clearing her throat. She is not sure how to start the conversation.

"Did you see any of the papers yesterday?" she starts tentatively. "There was something that really concerns me."

Bella is quick to guess where she is going.

"Are you thinking of the piece about Auberon?"

"So you have seen it?"

"I have."

There is a pause between them, they are both hoping the other will start the awkward conversation.

"It is terrible," Evelyn braves the silence. "They can write anything nowadays without having any proof or evidence."

"Yes, this is what I am worried about too."

"It must be dreadful for Auberon; my heart goes out to him." The old lady is getting into her stride, feeling that Bella might not be one of those #Me Too fighters, but she cannot be sure.

"It must be dreadful for Auberon, yes," says Bella, "but what if it is true and he is one of those types of men?

"I can't believe that, can you?"

"That was my first reaction too, but how can you be so sure? We never entirely show our faces to our colleagues in the theatre, do we? Have you ever worked with him before?" asks Bella.

"I regret to say I never had the opportunity. Sometimes we came close to being in a play together but it never happened. But you have worked with him, haven't you?"

Bella sighs deeply, "Yes, many years ago at the start of my career…"

"And?"

"And nothing. I never noticed any misconduct nor ever heard any rumours."

"You see, and you were just the kind of pretty young innocent this sort of thing could have happened to."

"It could have and it did, but not with Auberon."

The two women are looking at each other searching for some answers. They know this is the moment when they should unite, but it isn't easy.

"What do you think will happen now?" asks Evelyn.

"I have absolutely no idea."

"Do you think the others all know about it? Storm is very quiet today — after last night's debacle it is no surprise. I probed her a bit but I am sure she has not seen or heard anything."

"Maybe it will just go away. If no further details emerge," says Bella in a hopeful voice. "Tomorrow's news could be something different."

"I really hope so. I must leave you now to get ready and make yourself beautiful."

"Yes, it takes longer and longer nowadays," says Bella and stares at her image in the mirror.

Evelyn's hand is on the door when Bella says unexpectedly: "Are you all right darling? We never seem to talk nowadays."

Evelyn turns back, slightly surprised. "Yes, thank you I am fine."

"Maybe we could have lunch together one day. What do you think?" says Bella without removing her gaze from the mirror.

"That would be very nice."

"Only if you have the time," adds Bella.

Evelyn has to supress a smile. "Yes, yes, I do have the time."

"That's settled then," says Bella.

Evelyn leaves the dressing room, wondering whether Bella will remember that she's proposed lunch to her?

In their dressing room, Storm doesn't notice that Evelyn is distracted. She is so absorbed in her thoughts that the world around her is a closed book. Not only is she upset that she didn't get the job, but she is also concerned about her relationship with Gabriel. Is it a relationship? Does he think of it as such? Or is it just a fling that doesn't even seem to last as long as the run of the play.

Even though Gabriel stayed the night at her place and then they had lunch, it seemed to Storm that he couldn't wait to get away from her. The lunch could have been the last token in their romance. Suddenly, she feels that the whole play is worthless, her success in it pointless.

How could it be that everything that made her happy before is suddenly disappearing in a mist? She must concentrate on the performance — it is time for beginners to get on the stage. After yesterday's disaster, when she was responsible for delaying the show, she must be perfect tonight.

In the shared dressing room with Evelyn during the interval, the only time that Storm has a proper break, they are both sitting on their chairs looking at themselves in the mirror — usually the most interesting view in a dressing room — when Evelyn starts talking without looking at her.

"Do you know anything about the Auberon problem?"

"The Auberon problem, is that a physics question?" says Storm surprised, "because I've always been crap at physics."

Evelyn looks shocked. "No, I am talking about the rumours that have hit the newspapers about Auberon. It is serious."

"What rumours?"

"Several papers carried an article about a woman who accuses Auberon of inappropriate sexual behaviour."

"Our Auberon?"

"Yes, who else?"

"I am sorry, I just can't imagine it. He's such a sweetheart."

"Indeed. But does that mean that he must be innocent?"

"I don't know, I really can't think about this now — the second half is starting, I can't cope with anything like that clogging my mind."

Evelyn feels guilty and maybe a little unprofessional as well.

"I am sorry, I shouldn't have told you in the middle of the show. But soon everybody will know anyway, you'll see."

During the second act Storm is watching Auberon intently but everything seems normal — until the scene when Uncle Vanya talks about his ruined life. Auberon usually has tears in his eyes, but tonight, his eyes are dry. He gives a completely professional performance — the audience will be moved as much as any other night — but Storm can detect the difference. Something is dead inside the fine actor even though he is going through the motions.

He is still giving a great performance, thinks Storm; he is a wonderful actor. But could it be true? Could he be a predator? Suddenly, Storm has a flashback to when she is dancing with Auberon in Gabriel's flat on the night of the company's party, and

Auberon lightly touches her breast, more than once. No, this is stupid it will have been by accident, in the heat of the dance. But once the thought is there, she finds it difficult to erase.

Between scenes, Storm can feel a change of atmosphere. Gabriel and the stage manager are in an intimate conversation, and when Auberon passes them they suddenly stop. In another corner the dressers are whispering to each other.

Gabriel must know something, yet he's never shared it with me, thinks Storm. Then she sees Gabriel going into Bella's dressing room; that hasn't happened for a while. Everyone knows something but nobody is talking to me. Then Storm is a bit ashamed. After all she is not the story here. Does anybody think about how Auberon feels? Is anybody talking to him? No, he is standing in his usual off-stage place in the wings. He never goes into his dressing room during the play — his concentration is completely on the performance.

After the show is finished, everyone scurries home. There is no chat in the corridor, no invitations to the pub; it is as if the cold wind from outside had suddenly blown its way into the theatre. No one knows what the next step is going to be.

Storm is only a few yards beyond the stage door when she hears running steps behind her. It is Gabriel. "We must talk," he says. " Let's pop into the pub."

Storm is delighted to be asked. Maybe he wants to know more about her nearly missing the show. Or maybe it is about Auberon. In this general chaos she and Gabriel could form an island and let the tempest blow over, while they hold on to each other.

But this turns out to be just a shallow romantic dream. Gabriel seems sincere when he speaks.

"It was wrong of me to stay over at your place the other night. I've been feeling guilty ever since and I thought I should speak to you as soon as I could."

"Why are you feeling guilty? That is a useless sentiment," says Storm trying to sound the mature one in the relationship.

"Look, I want to be fair to you. I do have a long-standing girlfriend. We have had our ups and downs but it looks like I am going to commit to her. It surprises me too but that is what's happening."

Storm is silent. She feels the hurt but she cannot express it in words.

"What we had was lovely, but I think it is time for me to be the responsible one," he continues, just to avoid the silence. Storm would be laughing out loud at the word 'responsible' if she wasn't so utterly miserable. Somehow the word lovely hurts as well.

"You are so young — goodness, it is your first job...these things happen." Now he is floundering. "You will get over it in no time."

The anger is rising in Storm…He throws me these clichés…I deserve better than this… She still does not say anything. The tears are prickling her eyes, but she does not want them to spill out.

Gabriel keeps talking about the distorted pictures the theatre creates between individuals; he goes on and on. Storm doesn't even listen anymore. All she knows is that it is over after it has hardly begun, and she is feeling broken inside.

There is silence for a bit, then it is she who breaks it. "Let us go home now, we have a show to do tomorrow."

She reaches for her scarf and starts to roll it around her neck, but the stupid accessory just gets tangled up and Storm feels pathetic and laughable. She still doesn't cry; she will save that for the privacy of her room. She only regrets that she does not have the guts to tell him what a bastard he is.

Tension Growing

Bella wakes up in a good mood and feels empathetic towards the world. For a few days, nobody has mentioned Auberon's name. All seems to be quiet in the media. Bella remembers that she suggested lunch for Evelyn. Tomorrow would be as good a day as any, she thinks. She has Evelyn's mobile number, though the old lady told her that she often forgets to switch it on. Today must be a good day, because Evelyn answers the phone.

When Bella suggests lunch for the following day, there is a pause and Evelyn says she cannot make tomorrow. There is an obvious silence, and the statement needs an explanation.

"I have a hospital appointment tomorrow. It is just some test results," says Evelyn.
"I am sorry, I didn't know you had to have tests."
"Well, at my age things do crop up."
"Suddenly, Bella feels in a generous mood. "Would you like me to come with you?"
"That is very kind but…"
"No buts, I will come. What time is the appointment?"
"It is at twelve noon."
Now Evelyn has an urge to elaborate: "My granddaughter was supposed to be coming with me,

but she has exams, so at the last minute she's had to cancel."

"I didn't know you had a granddaughter in this town. Anyway, you must tell me about her tomorrow. So, that's settled. Is it the big hospital building at the corner of the main road?"

"Yes," comes the uncertain answer.

"I'll see you there ten minutes before." And Bella puts down the receiver before she changes her mind at her own unexpected philanthropy.

She has her shower, dresses and settles down to listen to the eleven o'clock news.

Among the headlines she hears something about an actor denying all accusations. She stops breathing for a moment—she is listening with all her sinews.

Finally, at the end of the news bulletin comes the crushing information: *Two more women have come forward accusing Auberon Hayman, the renowned actor, with inappropriate sexual behaviour. One of the women rang a popular breakfast programme on television to make her complaint about the actor, the other alleged victim had written to one of the daily newspapers. Neither is willing to give their name. The actor denies all wrongdoing.*

Bella's heart sinks—this can only end badly. Either Auberon is guilty, which is horrible to think about or he is innocent—and how would he be able to prove it?

In either case there will be a scandal, which will almost certainly impact on the production.

She decides that she cannot be a coward anymore. Tonight, she will go to Auberon's dressing room and have a word with him. At least she will know more about the situation, and maybe can give some support to her colleague.

Storm is into the last ten minutes of her morning run in the nearby park. Now, in the daylight, everything is clear; it is inconceivable how she got so hopelessly lost the other night. Running, while listening to her music through her earphones, is the one break she has from thinking about the confusing events of the last few days. When she is not running, she is troubled. As the time for the performance approaches, she feels elated, then disappointed.

It is drizzling, and her woolly hat is getting very damp. The path is muddy and her trainers are slipping and sliding. Her leggings are getting sprayed with mud and, for once, she finds it difficult to tell herself that all this is a healthy activity. It is all so miserable.

At last, she is at her front door. Inside, she removes her trainers and runs up the creaking stairs. At first, her room feels warm but she's hardly removed her scarf and hoody when she realises that the place is cold. That pathetic gas heater doesn't do much. She considers going back to bed but she remembers she hasn't fed the mice yet. She goes up to the cage but she can only see one of the mice. Which one? She could never differentiate between the two, and for this reason they were both called Mimi. Now Mimi Two was missing; in fact it could be Mimi One. Storm opens the cage door, and then she sees a little body at the bottom of the cage. Little pink legs pointing into the air. Mimi One is no more. Storm is quite taken aback. What is she supposed to do? Call a vet? Or just dispose of the body? Both seem wrong to her. She quickly closes the cage door, collapses on the nearest beanbag, and starts sobbing.

She doesn't understand it. Why? When she'd moved in, she was annoyed with the mice; then she thought they were quite amusing; and then she started caring for them. And now, one is dead. Like everything else in this wretched town, it starts well then it dies. She sobs even more.

After a while she pulls herself together, finds a plastic bag and removes the remains of Mimi One. Mimi Two is now promoted to the position of just Mimi. The trash needed to be taken out anyway and that is where the story ends.

The room seems a bit warmer now, and Storm decides to look at her messages and social media posts.

Even before she can open anything, news and notifications are all over her screen.

The scandal is not going away! screams one. *No matter how famous you are, you can't get away with abusive behaviour.*

Auberon's picture is everywhere. People are commenting on the news; most of them are unkind and cruel. It is clear that he is being condemned before any investigation, and there is no mention of a criminal trial.

Storm feels that what is in front of her cannot be all invention. Auberon must have done something that resulted in these women still hurting after so many years. What seems unacceptable is that Auberon was in a position of power — he was famous and admired, and he exploited that power. Those girls felt they wouldn't have a chance of being listened to. Thank God, it is different now.

Storm thinks how lucky she is that she is young now, when girls and women are less afraid to speak. She has the confidence to speak up and she knows that she would never put up with being treated as a sex object. But the perpetrators must be punished. Just because she likes Auberon now, he must not get away with behaviour like that. She feels angry but not sure how much of this anger can be shown in the theatre in this company. For the first time during the run she isn't looking forward to tonight's performance; it fills her with trepidation.

Before going to her dressing room, Bella makes her way to see Auberon. She crosses the stage with a heavy heart; Auberon's dressing room is at the opposite side of the stage from hers. The empty, half-lit set has a gloomy atmosphere, the only light coming from the prompt corner. The stage manager's lighting board blinks lazily. It is as if everything is sleeping, waiting for Prince Charming to come with the magic kiss. Each and every actor will play that part, giving their magic kiss to bring the set alive.

Bella crosses the stage on tiptoe, so as not to make a noise, which is senseless at this moment but she does it anyway. She takes a deep breath in front of Auberon's door, then knocks. The voice from inside comes after a longer than usual pause. "Come in."
Bella enters.

Auberon is just getting up from the couch where he was obviously having a rest. He looks pale and drawn. But on surface, always the gentleman: "Bella, how nice to see you. I mean off stage for a change." He points to the chair for her to sit down.
"I came in early. It is so peaceful here, I thought I'd have a cat nap."

Bella sees no point in making small talk. "How are you doing Auberon?"

He doesn't answer straight away; after a long sigh he comes to the point too. "You know none of it is true. You have known me for a long time. You must know that this is not me at all."

"But how could this happen to an innocent person? You must fight it. You must prove them wrong."

There is a bitter smile on his face now "And how can I do that? It is my word against the accusers; in today's climate is anybody going to believe me?"

Bella is lost as to how to give any comfort, but she feels that her presence at least gives some solace.

Auberon is looking for words, then at last he asks: "How is the rest of the company taking it, what do they say?"

Now Bella can answer with honesty. "You know, I haven't talked to anyone about you, I don't think that the company is fully aware of what is going on."

"I wish I could believe that. More like no one dares to take a stand, one way or the other. Don't think I blame them, I totally understand."

It is Bella's turn again to say something comforting. "Is there anything we can do for you?" Truthfully, she cannot imagine what it could be.

"Thank you, I appreciate your offer. Maybe ...maybe just that you say publicly that... No nothing, it would be harmful for you. At the moment, I don't think there is anything."

"Have a good show," says Bella and slips out of the dressing room.

On the corridor she bumps into Gabriel who sees her leaving Auberon's dressing room.
"How is he doing?" he asks.
"How do you think? Like a rat in a trap."
"What will be the outcome?"
"I have no idea, and the worst is, I don't think we'll ever know the truth."
"Even if I knew, I couldn't defend him."
"Why not?"
"I am a man."
"And?"
"Any man who speaks up for his friend is considered insensitive, a woman hater and a fiend."
"Do you think any of it is true?" asks Bella.
"I'd like to believe that it isn't, but you know, he has been famous for enjoying young people's company, coaching some; maybe the temptation was too much."

A dresser is passing them hurriedly and they stop talking. People whispering on the corridor is not a healthy state for a company. They both make their way to their respective dressing rooms.

While changing after the performance, Bella cannot take her mind off Auberon's plight. She remembers quite a few incidents that made her uncomfortable in her youth, but nothing as crass as the accusations against Auberon. She recalls one particular theatre in the provinces where the ageing artistic director was infamous for chasing young actresses round his office. Bella experienced his habit of appearing in the dressing room without knocking, hoping to catch the women in their underwear or less. Hence, they referred to the dressing rooms, as "undressing rooms" in the company.

I certainly hated it but was I damaged for life? Bella asks herself. It was all a bit of a joke in the profession. It would undoubtedly be a good thing, of course, if it didn't happen in the future.

Interrupting her thoughts, there is a knock on Bella's dressing room door. She is just changing into her street clothes, when she hears a cheerful "It is a girl, can I come in?"

The voice is familiar, yet Bella cannot place it. "Come!" she shouts. The door opens and a woman, elegantly but squarely dressed, comes through the door.
It takes a beat for Bella to recognise her. "My God Estelle, I don't think I have seen you since we left drama school."

"I was so afraid you wouldn't recognise me; it has been a long time," says Estelle just a tad too enthusiastic. "Actually, we did meet once after a recording of yours in the studio. I was there watching."

"How many years ago was that? No, I don't want to know," says Bella laughing. "What are you doing here anyway?"

"We live just a few miles out of the town, in the deep countryside, but I often come to this theatre."

Estelle congratulates Bella. She loved the production, and especially Auberon. There is an awkward pause, Bella does not want to talk about Auberon. She feels she ought to ask Estelle whether she is still acting or not, but what if she is? Then Bella should know about it — she doesn't want to be rude.

Estelle intuitively picks up the thought and tells Bella that she gave up acting ages ago. She has three children, and now she is a new grandmother.

Bella can't believe her ears. Grandmother? Estelle is only a couple of years older than her — she cannot be a grandmother. But Estelle is bubbling away.

"It is the greatest privilege on earth. I had my first daughter early and now she's just had a baby boy. I am crazy about him — it is such a pleasure — I look after him twice a week. Then Estelle stops, thinking perhaps that's enough about her family.

"So it doesn't clash with any work you might do?" Bella asks carefully.

"Oh, my family takes up all my time; that is my work now," comes the answer.

"It all sounds perfect. You don't miss the old acting then?"

"Well, if I could have been as good as you, maybe it would have been worthwhile. But yes, of course, I dreamt of having what you have, but I think it worked out for the best for me.

She writes her number down for Bella. "If you have any spare time while you are here, give us a call and maybe we can meet up. I could introduce you to master Damien—he is really gorgeous." With this, she sails out of the dressing room.

Bella stares into her mirror for a while, thinking of Estelle. She'll never have the thrill of the stage, but I shall never be a grandma. She pulls her coat on and turns off the light.

The Noose Tightens

Evelyn and Bella meet by the entrance of the hospital, both clutching a daily newspaper. They both look disturbed. Before Evelyn can say anything, Bella speaks.

"This morning we are concentrating on you. I know we have lots to say, but you must remain calm and give full attention to what the consultant has to say."

"I know you are right but..."

"No buts, we will talk after we have finished here."

Evelyn is not used to being instructed on what to do, except by theatre directors, but she is grateful for Bella's attitude. The worst thing about being alone is that she always has to make her own decisions; there is nobody to discuss or weigh up dilemmas with.

There are lots of people in the waiting room, and the usual hospital odour — medications mixed with cleaning materials — makes Bella nauseous. She hates hospitals. For a moment, she wonders how she came to volunteer to accompany Evelyn. But she pulls herself together.

Luckily, after a short wait, a bald gentleman with glasses calls Evelyn's name. He introduces himself as the hospital's consultant of neurology. Bella asks if she is allowed to accompany Evelyn and the doctor cheerfully says yes. "In fact, in our department we encourage the patient to have someone with them. Sometimes it is not easy to digest a diagnosis."

This does not bode well; on the other hand, the doctor's cheerful manner is encouraging. When the ladies settle opposite him, the doctor puts various scans of Evelyn's brain onto a lit panel.

"Here are the photographs we have taken," says the doctor, and while Bella can't banish the thought 'I wouldn't use them for Spotlight, ha-ha', she assumes a grave expression. When she glances at Evelyn, she notices that she looks much older in broad daylight than in the theatre, and seems pale and nervous.

"The good news is that there is nothing wrong with your brain. The experience you had is not rare, but naturally very frightening. It has a proper medical name: TGA, meaning Temporary Global Amnesia. It usually occurs in the over fifties age group and it can occur again or, with a bit of luck, never again."

Then the doctor turns to Bella. "However, we are concerned by the high blood pressure of your mother. Does she have it checked regularly?"

"I am not actually..." starts Bella, but Evelyn interrupts: "I am often away from my home working, and I don't go to the doctor's much." She is rather proud of this.

The doctor speaks to Bella again: "It is important that she has her blood pressure monitored."

Evelyn is getting angry. She is sitting right across from this doctor — why is he not speaking to her directly? It is so patronising. Especially now that he's said that her brain works perfectly well.

The doctor says he will write a letter to Evelyn's GP; meanwhile, he gives her a prescription to keep her blood pressure at bay.

The ladies leave the hospital relieved.

There is a small café near the hospital where they sell Italian coffee and croissants.

"You can't imagine how much England has changed," says Evelyn. "In my early days in Rep there was nowhere to have a decent cup of coffee in the provinces."

"Now you can't move for coffee shop chains," says Bella.

"Oh well, but they mostly sell American rubbish coffee." Evelyn nearly starts on her favourite moan, that all bad things originate in America.

They sit down at a quiet corner table.

"I didn't know that you had a granddaughter and living in this town!" Bella starts the conversation. "What a coincidence."

"Well, it was a surprise to me too. I didn't know she was here."

"How come?"

"It is a long story. I haven't seen her since she was a toddler. Unfortunately, my daughter and I are estranged and have been for many years."

"How sad. I didn't mean to pry…"

"That is all right. At the moment, I am delighted I have a granddaughter I never thought I would have. We are working on the relationship."

Bella is thoughtful, "It is so extraordinary, the theatre. We live in each other's pockets for a while and yet we don't know anything about each other. Then we part and we forget how close we were."

"Yes, that is true."

Now Evelyn wants to be brave too. "You never wanted children?"

Bella takes a deep breath. "I guess that is a long story too; it was never a conscious decision, it just happened or rather it didn't happen. Both myself and my husband had tests, they couldn't find anything wrong, the years were running by, busy years, and then it was suddenly too late."

There is silence. Both women have something at the forefront of their thoughts, but who is going to approach it first? Then almost at the same time they speak: "Have you seen the papers today?!"

Evelyn has waited for this moment to discuss the matter. "The papers are full of the Auberon scandal. There are pictures of him on the front pages, and more, from different periods of his life, inside the paper. The headlines are screaming of disgrace and the end of a distinguished career. The articles contain descriptions of the behaviour the women are accusing him of. It is just too awful."

"Unfortunately, the stories are very similar," says Bella, "which makes them more believable. Allegedly, he often took some young woman for a drive, who was thrilled to be in the car of the famous actor. He would drive somewhere quiet where he would stop and start fondling the girl and forcing her hand to hold his penis." Bella forces herself to utter the words.

"You think it can be true?"
"That is utterly disgusting," continues Bella "inexcusable".
"If it is true." Evelyn shakes her head "They have to prove it."
"How can they prove it? Presumably, there were no witnesses."
"How come there were no rumours going round the theatre companies?" Evelyn takes the line of the defence. "As far as I understand, they were all young women who would have liked to enter the profession; maybe they were his fans."
"I cannot believe that; it is just too crass."
"Eight of them came forward."
"Why are they withholding their names?"
"I don't know, but it seems the accusers have no profit in the revelations. They just want to speak the

truth, and maybe make sure that in future women will not be afraid to speak up if anything like this happens to them."

"They didn't have to get into his car," murmurs Evelyn, somewhat aware that she might be on the losing side.

If Evelyn is unconvincing as the defence, Bella is just as uncertain as the prosecution. Yet, she knows that she has to be strong—women have to stick together to change the horrible centuries-old culture, which accepts the abuse of women.

"What do you think is going to happen? I mean to us, the production?" asks Evelyn.

Suddenly, reality slaps Bella in the face. It may be the end of the play and the end of the transfer to London. That is painful for her in many ways. Do they all have to pay for the mistakes that Auberon made?

There are no answers to any of those questions. They will have to wait and see what happens in the theatre tonight.

There is a heavy atmosphere during the performance. Nobody is gossiping in the corridors; nobody wants to come across Auberon in the wings.

They all go through the motions of the play and scurry back to their dressing rooms. Now, everybody knows about the scandal, from the lighting man to the stage-door keeper. The company is holding its collective breath.

It is hardest for the people who are acting with him. Should they show sympathy or judgement, or should they just pretend that everything is normal? Should they chat about everyday matters, or should they remain silent? It is a bit like a bereavement, when nobody is quite sure how to behave.

In the interval, Michael appears and visits every dressing room. He starts with Bella, as hierarchy demands; it should be Auberon, but on this occasion he is avoiding his leading man.

Michael seems to be in a hurry; he wants to have got round to everyone by the end of the interval. There is no small talk. He comes to the point:

"I am sure you are aware of the unenviable situation that this company finds itself in. The board of directors would like to hear from individual members of the company, so there will be a meeting tomorrow morning at eleven o'clock in the green room. Bella, it is important that you're there. We will discuss how to approach the future, how to handle the press, and so on. Forgive me, I am not stopping to chat, I must tell the others. Obviously, Auberon will not be at the meeting."

Michael makes his way from dressing room to dressing room. When he leaves, Storm and Evelyn, the old lady, look shell-shocked.

"I have been in the business for more than fifty years and I have been in some challenging situations but this one is more awkward than any. I suppose they will close the show, even though Auberon is the best Vanya ever."

Storm's mouth is curving downwards; she is not so much shocked as angered.

"That is the only sensible thing to do. No matter how many years have passed, if you are guilty, you must be punished."

"And how do you know he is guilty? Were you there?" Now Evelyn is angry as well. She goes on: "Even if he is guilty, everybody deserves a second chance. And there is such a thing as forgiveness, not just in religion but in humanity."

"Well, you can only forgive somebody who admits his guilt. I haven't heard him making a statement regretting anything, have you?" Storm is unshakable.

At that moment, the stage manager calls for Act Two beginners and they have to abandon their argument. But it hangs in the air like some unpleasant odour seeping in from an unknown place.

In the wings, Bella is hanging on to Gabriel's hand and he squeezes her fingers. She translates this as we are in this together; do not fret; be strong. She feels a bit better but only for a moment, then her thoughts are on the possible outcomes. All scenarios seem to be bad for her. Let's just get through the play tonight, she thinks.

After the curtain call, backstage empties in the shortest time ever. The stage door keeper, a young woman, walks through, checking the dressing rooms, switching off the odd light. Tonight, she doesn't have to hurry anyone along on account of them still having a glass of wine with some visiting friends. Everything is dark and empty.

Well before eleven o'clock, the whole company is sitting stiffly in the Green Room. Even Storm is there on time. The tables have been pushed aside and there is a circle of chairs in the centre of the room.

"The therapy can begin," murmurs Gabriel, as he sits down next to Bella.

Michael comes in, followed by two men in suits. The company has never seen them before but they guess they are from the theatre board or maybe the local council. Michael never introduces them, and they don't say a word during the entire meeting.

"Thank you all for coming," starts Michael hesitantly. There are a couple of issues to talk over and we would like your input. He pauses, but this bunch of normally chatty thespians are quiet, holding their breath.

"There are some decisions to be made, and even if we don't present a united front, which I am guessing is possible, I don't want you to hear the outcome from somewhere else, like the press, for instance."

"The situation with Auberon Hayman is untenable for the theatre and the likelihood is that we have to close the play. Even an old film of his that was supposed to be shown tonight has been taken off by the BBC."

There is silence. Nobody wants to be the first to speak.

Now that Auberon is not present, Bella is next in the theatre pecking order. Michael turns to her: "Do you agree that we have no alternative?"

Bella feels now she ought to put up some fight for the company. "Could somebody take over the part, maybe?"

"We did talk about that, but, as you know, we have no understudies, and the remaining run of the play is less than two weeks. The role of Vanya is considerable, and just to come in for a few days would not be right."

Suddenly a voice that sounds familiar but not well known to them pipes up. The dear old lady who plays the nurse and never talks to anybody — just smiles with an angelic smile, starts talking.

"I am sorry, I don't quite understand. Has Mr Hayman been charged with anything or are we punishing him on account of the newspaper articles? Is this trial by media?"

There is stunned silence. The little stout lady dared to voice some of their thoughts. They realise they've never heard her voice, apart from her few lines on stage.

Michael is in the chair, so he has to answer. "I am afraid if we don't act now, we show that we disbelieve the complainers, and this is precisely the legacy we must fight against. We must give weight to the people who are complaining, who have been victims for a long time."

"A long time, exactly." — Now Evelyn is braver as well — "Why didn't they speak out for all those years, why now?"

The actor, who plays the professor, is respected by everyone. When he starts speaking, they all think he will defend Auberon. His words are weighed carefully, a bit slow to emerge but the meaning is crystal clear.

"It is exceedingly difficult for us all not to think of our personal situation. How much it means to us if the play closes. But I think, for the moment, we must consider that we are all under scrutiny. Are we putting our selfish reasons before the greater good, which is that a certain type of behaviour must be stopped, not just in the theatre but everywhere else? Of course, a famous actor will be more in the limelight and exploited by the papers than a bank manager. In this instance, we cannot wait for the accused to be proved guilty, we have to show that we are with the women who suffered in the past."

There is a chill in the room. If their kind colleague thinks this way, there isn't much point in arguing.

Michael continues in a similar vein: "I would like to point out that we are not here to decide whether Auberon is guilty or not; we are here to make a policy for the theatre and, more precisely, for this production. Social media is full of attacks, with gory details, and local people do not want a sexual predator in their theatre. In fact, they plan to organise protests in front of the theatre. So we need to act."

"In that case we have no alternative but to close the production," says Gabriel. "From what I am hearing here, I understand that if we show support for Auberon, we will all be tainted."

Storm springs to her feet and speaks with anger: "No, no, it is not about protecting ourselves. It is our job to make sure that nothing like that, the sort of thing Auberon is accused of — and we have no reason to think that the women are all lying — or anything similar, would happen to anybody again. That is the point of the whole movement, and not the individual stories."

"To be practical about it, we think we have to close the show," Michael continues. "We can still play tonight, as there is no time to inform our audience, but if anyone feels strongly that there should be no performance please say so."
Another embarrassed silence.

Then Storm speaks again. "I think we should abandon the show now. Don't you think it would be awkward to perform tonight?"

Evelyn thinks that when she was Storm's age she would not have dared open her mouth in a meeting like this.

Now it is Bella's turn: "Let us play at least one last time; then we can say a proper goodbye, not just to the whole crew but to our characters as well. I am assuming we can wave goodbye to the West End transfer?"

"Oh yes, there will obviously be no transfer of the production. It was going through very much on the strength of Auberon. His name is a big draw. At the moment, the producers are not looking at a change of cast."

Michael is speaking rather fast, as if he wants to get the whole sordid affair over with.

The silent crowd suddenly becomes noisy. They are all speaking at the same time.

"That is hard to take."

"God, that is really awful."

"My agent just turned down a lucrative job because of the play going to the West End."

After the initial shock, now it's personal, and hurting them all.

Eventually Gabriel speaks. "Well, then, even more reason to play tonight. We have a sold-out house; we don't want to disappoint them. It is enough that we are paying for the sins of Auberon—we don't want to hurt the audience as well."

Everybody looks at Storm. She just shrugs.

"Fine, we'll see you all tonight, and I'll obviously inform Auberon of the outcome." With this, Michael turns sharply and makes his way to the door. The two suits follow.

Finale

The last night of a theatre production is a bitter-sweet affair. The close community has spent so much time together that they've almost become a family, and, with the last show, it is time to say adieu. Each member has a different path ahead; some are happy to move on, others are regretting the end of a period of their lives.

This time it is all different. Nobody is ready to leave. Nobody has thought about the next step. Now, with the transfer cancelled as well, this last night is a sad event.

There is no gossiping in the corridors. Everybody's effort goes into giving their best performance of this production.

The atmosphere in the dressing room shared by Storm and Evelyn is a bit icy. It was clear at the morning meeting that they take different positions in the current crisis. Evelyn would like to play on till the end of the run, but Storm sees clearly that the situation is untenable. Personally, she thinks this is the right way to act if the theatre wants to put an end to the humiliation of women.

"Evelyn, you have to see that this is the only way the theatre can act." Storm would like to persuade the older actress. "You think this is easy for me? This production meant more to me than to anybody else. It was going to be my 'calling card' if we'd have made the West End."

"Exactly," says Evelyn, adjusting her black headdress in the mirror. "Why should you be punished for something that is not your fault? Why should you be collateral damage?" Evelyn is proud of this modern term.

"Unfortunately, this is the price we have to pay and I am willing to pay it."

Storm stands up with a heavy heart. She has to go on stage feeling that she is leaving not only Sonia behind but also her infatuation with Gabriel too. The happiness that relationship gave her and then the bitter disappointment, all within such a short time will become history now. But while it lasted it made her so alive!

She makes her way to the wings.

Auberon is already standing in the wings as he always does and Storm goes up to him and hugs him. She feels ashamed — is she a hypocrite, is she a cheat? But it was such a spontaneous gesture that it was too late to avoid it. Is Auberon a bad man? Maybe, but he is a wonderful actor, and they must not spoil this last night.

The performance is highly charged; perhaps the audience does not notice anything unusual but the actors on stage feel emotional. This time the emotions are not of their characters but their own.

Gabriel and Bella connect like they did in the first few performances. Their last embrace is long. Gabriel doesn't let her go—he squeezes the breath out of her with his bear hug, and Bella would like the moment to last forever.

At the curtain call, Auberon has tears in his eyes. He leaves the stage very fast, nearly colliding with Michael who comes to say goodbye to the company. Auberon doesn't turn back. Michael speaks only a few words thanking everybody for their hard work.

Finally, they are all saying their goodbyes. It is reminiscent of a funeral. Gabriel goes round, giving hugs to all; he even goes up to Evelyn and kisses her on the cheek. She blushes and returns the hug. Some of the cast shake hands with the stage crew, the lighting man and the stage managers. Then they disappear from the stage one by one. The stage is empty, the scenery and the props are all dead, they have no meaning without the live players.

Bella makes her way to Auberon's dressing room, before she goes to change. She knocks on the door; Auberon is sitting in front of his mirror staring into it. Bella speaks with a slight tremor in her voice.

"I just wanted to say goodbye personally, Auberon. I really hope that it will all be sorted out and we can still go to the West End."

"Not much chance of that," comes the reply.

"Take care of yourself," she says, and she is through the door. She didn't have the courage to say I don't believe the things they say about you, or ask him what really happened. In honesty, she cannot decide where the truth lies.

When Bella leaves, Auberon stares into the mirror. He cannot believe what is happening. He is shell-shocked. Everything has happened with such tremendous speed. One minute, the talk was of his outstanding performance as Vanya, — admittedly only in limited circles — the next minute he is a pariah, the worst kind of person, an abuser. And this has become known to everybody, regardless of age and interest in the theatre.

Auberon wants to be honest with himself. Have I done those things they are accusing me of? Yes, I have. Some of them. They didn't seem important, just a little amusement. And they were different times. I thought the girls were pleased — some definitely came back for more. Why did they do that if it was such a terrible experience for them?

And what about the future? It looks bleak. Is it possible that his entire career is over? Is that a proportionate punishment, that for the mistakes he made many years ago, some he hardly remembers, his whole life's work and achievements are finished forever? He guesses that he is unemployable. For how long? The tortured image in the mirror has no answers to any of the questions.

After Bella has changed, and before she packs her things, she runs up to Storm's and Evelyn's dressing room. The two women are sitting on their chairs in front of their mirrors. Storm is bending over her dressing table, arms covering her face, and she is sobbing. Bella looks at Evelyn, surprised, and Evelyn just shrugs.

"I've tried to comfort her, but she just can't stop."

Bella goes to Storm and hugs her.

Storm looks up; her make-up is all smeared, her mascara running down her face. Suddenly she looks frighteningly young, at least to Bella.

"Yes, yes, I am stopping. I know I am being stupid..."

No, we understand," says Bella, "Only you were the one, you were so sure..."

"I know I was, no in fact I am. I am sure that we've all done the right thing, but now that it is all over, it is just so horrible, I can't bear it..."

"You can. You know when one door closes another soon opens." What a terrible cliché, thinks Bella and tries to do better. "Nobody can take away from you how good you were here as Sonia." Bella, doing her damned best to console her young colleague.

Storm quietens slowly, blows her nose and continues to pack her belongings. They try to carry on with a normal conversation.

"I didn't want to go without saying a special goodbye to you two," Bella says, still shocked by Storm's unexpected breakdown.

"That is sweet of you," says Evelyn. "Are you travelling tonight or staying over?"

"My husband is collecting me. We are driving back to London tonight. What about you?"

"I am going to take the train tomorrow. I am in no hurry," says Evelyn.

Storm joins in, as if nothing has happened. "And I will go on the same train. We'll go together Evelyn. I'll help you with your luggage," adds Storm. "Though I will have a small cage with me with my mouse."

"What? Your what?"

"I have a pet mouse, Mimi — it is very sweet."

"When did you buy a mouse for yourself?"

"I didn't actually; it is a long story, but I feel I can't leave her behind. It is worth taking, just to see my mother's face when I arrive! But still, it will be good to travel together."

Evelyn is surprised; she smiles at Storm. "That'll be nice." Then adds, in a mumbling bitter voice. "I am sure I shall never work again."

"We all feel like that when a job is finishing," says Bella smiling. "Except when you are as young as Storm. That is why you have the least reason to panic."

"Really, at the moment I feel just like Evelyn," says Storm gloomily. "Will I ever work again? I am angry that I am missing an opportunity to show what I can do. I am angry, but there are more important things to consider."

"Yes, it is a real shame for you," says Evelyn. "This part was a marvellous launching pad".

"I am not regretting the theatre's decision. We had to close—there was no alternative." The young woman is emphatic, but her voice is shaky, and there's a threat of returning tears.

"This is what we don't agree on," Evelyn sighs deeply. "Anyway, speaking personally, I don't know why I feel so useless when I am not working. After all, at my age, I could be happily retired and crocheting at home."

"Who retires in this business?" asks Bella.

"I often ask myself," continues Evelyn, "why am I fulfilled when I am working but feel like a waste of space when I am not? After all, it is not as if I am saving the world, being a doctor or a nurse. Who does it help if I am on stage, or deliver three lines in a television play? And yet..."

"It helps you, it is good for your mental balance, and that is all that matters," says Storm.

"Even when I played the big parts," Evelyn carries on, "how did that impact on the world?"

"Well, you gave joy to hundreds of people who were watching you," Bella reasons.

"I am convinced that there are only a very few magical actors who can claim that they gave some special experience to the audience, somebody like Olivier…and I think Auberon is in that category."

"It is a pity that he also belongs to another category, the sexual predator." Storm holds fast to her position.

"Listen, I am sure we will all have jobs soon. Let's keep in touch and let each other know," suggests Bella.

"I cannot get it into my head that people can condemn an artist on the strength of hearsay…Nothing has been proved, it could be all made up…" Evelyn shakes her head.

"But all the women are telling almost the same story—they couldn't have made it up. It happened at different times and different places, but his behaviour was the same." Bella seems to try to convince herself.

"Don't you see, how important this is?" says Storm. "We want to change it for all women who work in this industry and everywhere else. Men should not be able to get away with assaulting women anymore. That is the goal and for that we might have to sacrifice certain things in the short term."

"I have the feeling that we three are not going to solve the wrongs of the world. So, take care of yourselves," says Bella.

"Let's start a What's App group then we will know who is doing what," suggests Storm.

"What is that?" Evelyn is clueless.

"Don't worry I'll show you. I'll download it for you. You do have a smart phone, don't you?"

"It's a phone. I am not sure how smart it is."

"Well girls, take care of yourselves and I hope we see each other soon."

One more hug from Bella, and she is out of the dressing room.

Ten minutes later, she is leaving from the stage door. By the notice board stands Gabriel, as if he is waiting for something. They embrace once more. It is a long and tight hug. Then Bella notices Theo approaching. The two actors separate but Gabriel snatches Bella's hand and kisses it. Then she is through the door and into Theo's car.

"Sorry about that—it is all a bit emotional," says Bella.

Theo is smiling and mumbles, "Actors..." he puts her suitcases and a few boxes into the boot of the car and turns the key in the ignition.

Epilogue

From the News in Brief section in The Times.

The Metropolitan Police have decided not to press charges against the actor, Auberon Hayman, following complaints of inappropriate sexual behaviour. The Police said that after "thorough assessment we determined the information would not meet the threshold for a criminal investigation." Consequently, Mr Hayman will not be prosecuted.

*Last December he was ejected from the actor's union, Equity, and his role in the forthcoming film **Don't Look Back**, which was completed a year ago, was re-shot, with another actor.*